Dakshita Das is a civil servant who is a graduate of Lady Shri Ram College for Women.

Myself Meena, IAS is her debut novel.

MYSELF
MEENA, IAS

Dakshita Das

RUPA

Published by
Rupa Publications India Pvt. Ltd 2016
7/16, Ansari Road, Daryaganj
New Delhi 110002

Sales Centres:

Allahabad Bengaluru Chennai
Hyderabad Jaipur Kathmandu
Kolkata Mumbai

ISBN: 978-81-291-4028-9

First impression 2016

10 9 8 7 6 5 4 3 2 1

The moral right of the author has been asserted.

CONTENTS

PROLOGUE

My nana had once warned me about two types of pain in this world: physical pain that merely hurts, and an internal aching pain that changes you totally. He had also helpfully amplified that of all the pains in the world, it hurts the most when you land on your butt. Of course, he used the Hindi word for butt, which made it sound worse. The day I joined work it was as though he was around me, his words prophetically resounding. I had walked into a disaster. Sheer unadulterated disaster. In short, I had landed hard on my butt!

But my narrative of disasters and upheavals doesn't start at this job, it ends here. My tale started eons ago, when I was still an egg waiting to be fertilized. Along with Baba's sperm, truckloads of his unfulfilled dreams and ambitions were jammed into my DNA. I can well imagine Baba happily chortling at my birth 'here is what I could not be!' and hastily setting out to purchase encyclopedias and books and exam guides for me while other dads planned for diapers, baby milk and suchlike. Other babies sucked at their teething rings while I was handed a cloth book to chew. Other toddlers played with toys while I was put in front of a computer which ran an educational programme designed for tots. While other babies lay in their cots gurgling, I was put through what Baba termed 'share the view'. He'd take me for long walks in a backpack, and narrate whatever he saw: 'that's a little dog' or 'look at those big trees!' or 'did you hear that car?' All designed to give me endless vocabulary. This, in sum, was the general drift of my childhood.

Sweets were distributed in the neighbourhood the day I lisped my first sentence: 'Myself Meena, IAS.'

Tears poured down Baba's face even as he battled with my oh-so-wrong English while my normally unemotional ma too looked weepy. Yes, my destiny was doubtless shaped in her womb.

By hindsight, while Baba gave me several inputs, the one on common sense was missing. Therefore, once unleashed into the big bad world to make choices, its absence combined with providence really freaked me out. Thus, the point at which I am right now can only be surmised as the last chapter of my story i.e., The End.

But for you, the reader, let me begin at the very beginning.

1

ME, ALFA ROMEO

I entered my family at a time when Ma was harassed enough to not want another child. But for Baba it was a different story altogether. Inspired by the neighbourhood astrologer who forecast that things would change if Baba expanded his family, regardless of the child's sex, he looked at his newborn daughter with tremendous enthusiasm. Accordingly, I was viewed as an out-of-the-ordinary child born with a special destiny.

'I'll ensure she becomes a sarkari officer', was Baba's earliest thought—sarkari job being the ultimate goal for the average resident of Bareilly, aka us. Maybe that aspiration got interminably intertwined with what he was undergoing in his life at that precise point in time. In short, the district commissioner, his boss four times removed, was at his throat as the teeny tiny district health hospital Baba headed continually threw up death cases, one after the other. If it was malaria one day, then it was cholera the next, and then, lo and behold, chikungunya struck. So he was sandwiched between patients, their grieving kin and the hopping-mad district administration. It was clear that his life's ambition was that I grow up to bash up the world the way he was being bashed up! In a nutshell,

Baba wanted power!

Baba was a physician. He came from a good family which had no money. Mom came from a good family with money, which they didn't want to part with. So, existence was fairly hand to mouth for us. If a patient offered loads of vegetables as fees, we'd live off those. Else dal, roti and aloo were our staple fare.

Given my so-called special destiny, I grew up totally spoiled and guided by Baba's lenience, quite unlike my older sibling, Bhai; no housework for me while he was sent to fetch milk, buy vegetables and climb up the roof to release the air from our creaking water pipelines. I was expected to just study and perform well.

I went to a convent school with my better-off cousins. I wore their hand-me-downs, which was duly announced by them to all and sundry. Terribly humiliated early on in life, I tried making up for that with my good grades, which somewhat insulated me from their sneers and the mocking. You really can't run down a prized student, can you? Till the junior school, I was up on the stage year after year receiving prizes for excellence in academics. After each of my prize distribution ceremony, Baba would preen and strut like a peacock and advise others on how to bring up a brilliant child. 'Arre, Bhai saheb,' he'd tell his astrologer who had forecast my future, 'you are simply a genius!'

But sadly, shortly after, somewhere in middle school, hormones struck and I changed tracks. I sprouted pimples and a bust and an intense attraction for boys. My motto switched to 'You are young only once! If you follow all the rules, you'll miss out on all the fun'. Friends became more important than anything and, much to Ma's irritation, the intensity of the giggles from my room when my friends came over knew no limits. She'd also frown at the eye shadow and mascara I tried to experiment with. As for nail polish, whereas it was a huge 'no-no' for her, I'd try and put on a colourless shade in sheer defiance. Naturally, my grades began to slip.

It was clear that things had gotten out of control when the Physics teacher wrote a note home that read, 'the student lacks a scientific temperament'. I hid it from my parents. The big issue that loomed large in my life was how to tell Baba that I had completely lost the plot.

Luckily my parents never attended parent–teacher meetings. Baba felt they were an utter nuisance and also that star pupils needn't have worried parents! But I could sense him getting all worked-up by the time I reached Class 9, as there were no more prizes. At best I got one for the three C's, that is, courtesy, caring and compassion which was neither here nor there or because they didn't include subjects. My academic downfall was as certain as death and taxes!

I had confided in Sunita, my best friend, 'What to do, Sunni? Baba has dreams and I have no interest in Maths, Physics or Chemistry.'

'Just take the Board Exams,' Sunni advised. 'We're shifting to another system of grading from this year where we'll be getting A's and B's instead of numbers and no one will know the difference. Chalo, my chacha's son is waiting outside with his friend. We'll go out for a drive. Such fun, na? It's going to rain and a drive in the rain is really romantic.'

'Well …,' I tried protesting.

'Come, yaar,' she insisted. 'You know that he has the hots for you.'

So it was bye-bye to tuitions, hello to lots of mooning in

the rain and a permanent farewell to calculus which I never ever understood thereafter. After classes, Sunni and I'd be out of the school running into the waiting car. Her cousin would take us for long drives and, sometimes, movies which I'd otherwise never get permission from home to see. Nothing as such which can be termed promiscuous but fairly off the line and totally out of the syllabus as set for me by Baba.

My feeling of hopelessness and anxiety increased as the Class 10 Boards came closer. I just couldn't understand a thing. Even Hindi and English were torturous. All that poetry in Braj bhasha and Shakespeare in English. Lousy! Worse still, the wicked girls in class had nicknamed me Alfa Romeo after the famous sports car. I could be found running away from books and into the arms of Sunni's cousin faster that you could blink. It helped that we lived in a huge dilapidated bungalow for medical officers, which had a broken down back entrance. I'd leave the lamp on at night and slip away leaving Baba to think that his brilliant daughter was neck-deep in the world of academics while I partied like there was no tomorrow.

Close to the exams, it was Sunni's cousin who came to our rescue.

'Guide book le lo,' he advised, 'you'll understand well.'

So guide books became my new teacher. Terrified of disappointing Baba, I blocked hormones and doggedly tried to study. I had missed out a complete cycle of study and frankly didn't like a single subject. I turned for sympathy to Ma, an otherwise hazy figure in my life, who seemed to be merely cooking and washing.

'Ma, I don't like any subject…,' I hesitantly started.

'Tell that to your Baba,' was the terse rejoinder. 'He has filled your head with all this nonsense of becoming an officer.

Who'll marry you once you cross the age? And just look at you? You don't know how to cook or run a house and I suspect that the light you have on in the room at night is only pretence.'

Ouch! Ma seemed to know more than I thought. So, no looking for sympathy or a solution to my crisis there.

The boards loomed large but guess what! I was saved by totally unplanned circumstances. Nana fell ill and my mother's brothers discovered us all over again so that he could be shifted to our house and Baba could oversee his treatment. Baba was gloomy while Ma was happy to have her father home. I needed to give up my room for Nana; naturally that would harm my studies. And yes, it happily did! The papers were a haze in front of my eyes. Maths was a killer but someone had told us (was it the class teacher?) that you get numbers for the working as well, so I was hopeful of passing but not really of performing. True to expectations, the results were disappointing.

Baba blamed Ma and couldn't say so because he didn't want her angry. Ma, however, was smarter. She knew that he would blame her father's illness for my poor performance and happily regaled him with what I'd been up to in the last few months. The aunty who lived next door spilled the beans on me (why on earth was she keeping tabs on our house at late hours beats me). Ma had also got to know about Sunni's cousin and threatened me with dire consequences if I didn't begin housework. But it was tragic for Baba. He behaved like someone out of a Meena Kumari film: Baba neither shouted nor raged, he just looked broken, so utterly broken. I was ashamed. His dreams of watching me become an engineer with an MBA degree and then as an IAS (Indian Administrative Service) officer lay in shreds.

2

STUDY, STUDY, STUDY!

There appeared little choice but to shift to Humanities in Classes 11 and 12. I swore off boys. I figured out that Sunita was not really the best of friends to have. Education was merely timepass for her and I was getting bored of her constant references to her rich father, and just how much money he had and also her invariable jibing about how we didn't own a car or have a servant and lived in a shabby house.

With that looming fact, the smartest thing I could do at that point was to just stop wasting time and determinedly study, study, study. I also became friends with the kitchen and learnt my way with vegetables and masalas. In the far horizon lay the possibility that with good grades I could move to Delhi, and then enjoy life and live it to the fullest, compensating for the loss of good times at present.

Life moved on. Sunni got engaged to a rich timber merchant's son and could be seen in Page 3 parties draped over his arm. I turned to more academic company and was frankly very, very lonely. I was neither Sunni nor academic, I was supposed to be me and I didn't know what 'me' was. But my parents appeared relieved. Ma now had a helping hand in the house and could merrily boss over me. Baba was a wee bit more silent now, but his acceptance of the situation gave me less of a guilt trip.

3

I WANT OUT!

Seema, Sabina and I were the surprise toppers of our high school. Actually Sabina topping the Board exams was no great surprise. Her result was expected; she was really a nerd and a sneak and hid her bag of books even from me, purportedly her closest friend. She'd also won the state level award for her English essay on how to save the trees around our school. The trees were knocked down in any case but she was the winner of the gold medal, which was good for her CV. She did everything only for her CV.

Seema knew right from the beginning that she was beaten. She had to eventually move over to a local girl's college, if at all she were allowed to study further and was not married off to some loser from a town even smaller than the one we lived in. Both of them were my neighbours, and the new control mechanism which now ruled my life meant that the three of us would squeeze into a rickshaw and head for inter college. One of our brothers would cycle alongside as our bodyguard.

I moved notches up academically only by default: in the company of these two I could barely talk stuff beyond studies. They didn't even watch TV! Actually, I'm wrong; Sabina watched the National Geographic channel. Wow! Having shed most of my previous social circle, these were the only company my parents would approve of. Also, any day History and Political Science were easier subjects to rattofy than Maths and Science. One can't discount the fact that I was really desperate. Any more of that dratted place, our ramshackle house, Ma's disapproving looks and Baba's constant egging to be an achiever, and I'd jump into the nearest well. I needed a break, a good clean one, away from my family and Bareilly to discover myself.

4

HALLELUJAH!

God listened and I made it to a prestigious Delhi college. Hallelujah! Bhai resentfully dropped me off in Delhi with a trunk and other stuff and a limited amount of cash. At the girls' hostel gate he warned that I was here to fulfil a dream and not waste my time. Fat lot of attention I paid heed to that advice as I spotted a small-ish dhaba facing the entrance. Students lounged around the place, lit cigarettes in hand, downing cups of tea. Let me confess, after the all-girls schooling I had gone through, seeing boys in that dhaba was such utter joy!

Once hostel formalities were over, I literally ran around to explore the campus. Of course, I sneaked on a bit of lip gloss, which I was dying to since I'd reached Delhi. All the girls I had seen so far wore make-up here, unlike the regimented lifestyle that I had been leading in which kajal was the only cosmetic permitted by my parents.

'Hi!' said a bespectacled boyish person as I went out to fetch tea for myself from the canteen. 'I'm Sudhir. Geography honours. You've just joined college?'

Geography, oh my god! I thought. No one studies Geography. But being pretty much the first boy I was interacting with on campus, I swallowed my thoughts and simpered at him.

'I'm Meena, History. I'm from Mahila Girls College, Bareilly.'

'History, ha! Didn't get anything else, is it?' uttered Sudhir, much to my fury.

'Excuse me!' was my reaction. 'It's Geography that attracts all the dregs and leftovers. My dad says that History is a sure-shot scorer in the Civil Services Exam.'

'Civil Services Exam, haah? OMG, I'm with a serious type! God, I want your autograph, yaar. Sooo focused at this age. Can you imagine the headlines? Bareilly throws up a UPSC (Union Public Service Commission) winner. An IAS officer. Wah! Wah!'

Turning to another boy sitting next to him, he said, 'Yaar, Deepak, we'll have to befriend Meena. Maybe in her reflected glory we'll also become important.'

I can fortunately sense a taunt when I see one and was off in a huff leaving the two sniggering boys behind. Of course, I knew with a sinking heart that my goose was right royally cooked and that the UPSC tag would follow me wherever I went. I was an utter and total gobo!

As a silver lining to the dark clouds, my roommate seemed to be a nice girl. Malathi from Bengaluru, who was already in a nightie at 5 in the evening. The moment I entered the room she launched into simple day-to-day talk.

'Hi!' she said. 'I've chosen this side of the room near the window. I get up at 5 a.m. to study and need the light. Do you think we could work out an arrangement of room cleaning? One week I'll sweep and swab and the other week it can be your turn?'

Somehow, this basic detailing took my mind off the trauma

of the encounter with Sudhir and company. Malathi seemed more confident and focused on what she wanted to do with her life. I concluded that she would be an appropriate shield to my wavering mind and could also provide me the direction I may on and off need. She had a brother in the US working in the IT industry and was studying to go and join him. If you took away the perpetual smell of coconut oil, I think she was an overall okay type to share a room with.

We wandered down to the mess for tea and I told her of my disastrous encounter in the canteen. It was pretty clear to her that I was terribly upset by it.

'What's wrong with you?' Malathi reacted. 'You can't be conditioned by what other people say. If you want to do UPSC, you want to do it. Why feel guilty about it? In my entire family we're engineers and doctors and we know that we'll be so from birth. Should we feel guilty?'

Duly comforted, I concluded that I was in good company.

That first night though was tough in the hostel. Malathi slept off at 8, immediately after dinner, leaving the lamp on for me. I tossed and turned in bed running over the day's events, excitedly wondering what lay in store for me. It had been tiring, the travel, the new environment, the fact that I was now to be in charge of my life and take decisions. I got so wound up that sleep eluded me till early morning.

'Clang!' A sharp noise jarred me awake at 6 a.m. In the semi-darkness I figured out that Malathi was pushing off to the loo and a bath with her bucket and other paraphernalia. I turned over and dozed off but she was back sooner than I thought.

'The loos are FILTHY! Only if you reach there the first thing in the morning do you get a place you can use and bathe in. You'd better rush.' she warned. 'I've left my bucket in the second room on the right for you!'

So I hurried off, and in that semi-comatose state bathed in the bathroom clogged with ankle deep water; that's how my first day at college began.

The early few days actually passed in a haze. All I could figure out was that I needed money to buy books and hadn't the faintest clue how to ask Baba for it. To top it all, the hostel seemed to have a life of its own. Birthday parties had already begun, which meant not only late nights but also that I would be required to buy gifts (more money!), host a party and stuff while Baba would only talk about my preparations for the UPSC. I became gloomy. Malathi meanwhile seemed unaffected by this and moved on in her pre-determined groove where she woke up early, bathed, studied, had her breakfast, went for classes and studied more until she went off to sleep. Frankly, it appeared that the restless hormones which are normal in most people of our age had totally given her a miss.

Academically, it was pretty much evident on the first day itself that the teachers were so utterly uninspiring that they wouldn't really motivate me or anyone else in my class to great heights. The Ancient History teacher gushed at us 'Gooood Morrrrning! My name is Pinky Sharma and I wear Pink!'

Really?!

P. K. Das, the teacher who taught us Sources of History, lived up to his reputation by fixing afternoon tutorials for all the girls 'one-by-one' in his room. Ashutosh Sir intimidated us by informing that he was a permanent employee of the university and was drawing ₹80,000 as salary. Now, was that supposed to make sense to us? Seriously, the school teachers at Bareilly had been far, far better.

By the time the third class was over, I think I switched off totally, particularly when Seema Ma'am started on European History.

'The British... (pause)... they were very, very good, and you are not knowing how good they were for our India. They were being good rulers...'

This can't be Delhi education? I thought morosely.

'Why so lost?' asked the girl sitting on the decidedly uncomfortable bench next to me. She'd come in late for class and was dazzlingly attired in a pink tank top with oodles of lip gloss.

'Am I lost?' I reacted defensively.

'Suit yourself,' she retorted, 'I was only trying to be friendly.'

However, seconds later she offered her hand to me.

'I'm Priyanka. Let's start again. After all, we will be together in this for three years.'

I liked that. Priyanka, a slick city girl, had chosen to befriend me despite my Mahila College, Bareilly stamp. She eventually became my friend, philosopher and guide. I liked her for the fact that she never seemed to think beyond the minute, was ever-smiling (and, also, as I discovered, very prone to dangerous decisions). So Malathi became my guide when I needed motivation to pursue what I now firmly labelled as 'Baba's goal for me', and Priyanka catered to my devilish side, buried deep since my Class 10 Boards!

5

THINGS GO HORRIBLY WRONG

*H*istory is actually an easy subject to study. In fact, one really doesn't need classes for it. Priyanka had pretty early abandoned all pretence of even becoming vaguely familiar with the subject, intending to solely rely on the mug books and question banks. The only thing bugging her was the mandatory requirement of attendance. It was like really essential to cross the 75 per cent attendance benchmark.

'P. K. Das I'll manage,' she told me trustingly, 'Lech that he is. Will you tackle Pinky for me please because you are her star pupil?'

Star I undoubtedly was. Pinky Ma'am and I both came from Bareilly and that was reason enough for her to take me under her wings. There was also a scholarship which I could get if I did well in the first semester. So to be honest, I slogged. Malathi and I would be up at 5 a.m., to study, clang our way to the bathrooms and be the first in for our respective classes. All I needed was coconut oil and I'd be a Malathi clone!

So, I topped in the first semester. Baba would be thrilled I thought, and the scholarship would be mine. Pinky Ma'm had already cleared that bit for me. I sat in the library composing a happy letter to Baba. At last, it appeared, his dreams for me were taking shape.

'Hi, topper,' said a male voice. It was Sudhir, the Geography boy.

I'd been avoiding him like a plague, holding him and Deepak responsible for the dirty stories about me being a nerd floating around campus.

'You seem to have taken to academics like a duck to water. Chalo Bhai, ab UPSC bhi door nahin (Good, now UPSC is not too far away),' he said.

Obviously he had heard that I had got the first semester scholarship and I could sense the taunt in his words.

'Can't you find another place to sit?'

I retorted in a loud tone.

The librarian looked up and the boy beat a hasty retreat.

Priyanka was on a maiden visit to the library and overheard our interaction.

'What was that about?' she asked.

I was in tears.

'I hate that guy,' I said and launched into my encounter with him at the canteen when I had just joined college.

'Hmmmm,' commented Priyanka thoughtfully. 'What you need in fact is an image makeover. We need to seriously work on that. Once you are spruced up, no one will take cognizance of what those guys say. These ragged jeans and T-shirts and the Aunty type salwar kameezes won't do. Time for a new wardrobe, a visit to the parlour and loads of attitude.'

My heart sank. Apart from the attitude, everything else required money, and asking Baba for it was ruled out.

'Don't worry about the cash,' continued Priyanka, as if reading my thoughts, 'how do you think I manage? I get a mere subsistence allowance from home, yet you see me with the latest fashion and make up, don't you?'

'How...then?'

'Arre, when Priyanka is there, why worry! Today we'll bunk the afternoon tuition, and I'll take you shopping, my style!'

Bursting with excitement and curiosity, it was tough to pass time in class: what on earth would Priyanka work out? As it transpired, not a very good thing. I was introduced to the art of shoplifting! Priyanka was a veteran at it and whether a low-end shop or a swank establishment, she just could walk in and walk out with anything! I marvelled at her. Our first escapade was at the famous cottage emporium. According to Priyanka, if you could lift something here then you could be awarded a PhD in the art of shoplifting! We walked out, two small clutch bags richer. Next we were at the Khan Market after hitching a ride with a richie-rich type who looked as if he would happily paw us at the next red light. Luck didn't favour us that well in the Khan Market as the shopkeeper spotted us shoplifting and gave a chase of a lifetime. We escaped, but just about so. Adrenalin poured, we gave each other high fives. I was hooked, properly hooked.

Malathi sniffed disapprovingly at the new bag I swung under her nose. She disapproved further when she got to know that I had gone out with Priyanka. Apparently, the entire hostel knew that my friend was a confirmed shoplifter and now I was a part of her two-member gang. Ouch! Baba would weep if he got to know. Each time we spoke, he'd boost me by saying that once I hit big time by slogging-hard-and-becoming-an-officer, all our worries would be over. But, at this point of time, I was hugely besotted by Priyanka and her ways. And that cost me dear. My grades fell in a jiffy. By now a lot of people were sniffing disapprovingly at me, including my pet teacher Pinky. As for that creep who had triggered this off, Sudhir would look at me conspiratorially and wink as if he knew why I was sporting new stuff and appearing threaded and waxed, and plucked clean as a hen.

'Dropped the idea of UPSC, eh?'

He mocked and I nearly swatted him one with my new, stolen Hidesign bag.

6

THE CLIMBDOWN

*B*aba always said that it is easier to climb up than come down, but I proved him wrong. For me the downslide was faster and unfortunately painful.

The next few semesters were a nightmare. I couldn't shake off Priyanka. She had become a habit. I loved her for her butterfly ways and for her free spirit; she was what she was. Things had worsened because from the second semester we'd been given single rooms and I found it tough to dish out reasons to my inner disapproving self (and also Malathi) as to why Priyanka would hang out with me all the while. Expelled from the hostel in the second semester itself she simply moved into my room. She'd sleep during the day and party at night. The room would be filled with cigarette smoke which meant that Malathi for one boycotted it totally.

Guiltily, I would head home for holidays travelling by the unreserved coach (to save on the cost of ticket!) and Ma would be very vocal that I be brought back to study in Bareilly or better still, married off. After all, there were financial liabilities to discharge, including installments to be paid for a new house. In addition she didn't approve of my new appearance. Bhai had also been sneaking on me. He too had moved to Delhi and was lodging in a barsati while working in a law firm, and it appeared to me that he was doing more sleuthing on me than slogging it out in new job. Ma knew my weakness, that I lacked sense, or any sense of judgment and really craved glamour and excitement. She tried to caution me in her own way. Things worsened when Priyanka and her pal came home to spend the next Diwali with us. Ma found them in an inappropriate pose at night and threw them out. So I returned to college without friends, without an academic record and unhappy as hell. To boot, there was no romance in my life; no boyfriend, no casual fling, nothing to give that little pep and zing in life. Life, it seemed, was moving around in concentric circles, and I was losing on time while it raced by.

Do you know what it is like to just wistfully pass away time, living through one's so-called destiny, hating the subject you are studying and being written-off? I had begun so well and look where I had landed three years later. Often, I'd question things, why did my life periodically take such a roller coaster turn?

Deepak saw me sobbing into my History books in the library one evening. In any case I hated him because I think my problems had everything to do with him and his lovely friend Sudhir. I tried to wipe off my tears as he sat close and cleared his throat.

'I've been trying to find you all over.'

'To poke more fun at me?'

'No! No! Please, don't misunderstand me or us for that matter.'

'Really? You call this a misunderstanding? Considering that the entire college and its mother knows the minutest details of our very first conversation.'

I sniffed at him.

'Well,' he had the grace to look sheepish, 'but I didn't do the talking. You know how much I keep to myself.'

'What is it you want of me?' I took the conversation further, wanting to rid myself of the fellow.

Deepak took a deep breath and said, 'I'm moving on for further studies in Law to the US. I always wanted to be a lawyer. And don't run down Law the way you ran down Geography.'

He wryly remarked, evoking the memories of our first meeting.

I looked at him with new eyes. I'd known him to be a quiet sort who kept largely to himself but didn't know that he would crack it to one of the top US law colleges.

'Well, all the best,' I said to him, 'keep in touch if you can.'

'I will,' he replied, 'and you fulfill your dream too. You know, one can aim for the moon and get it too, just focus, the stars are waiting for you to pluck them.'

I liked that bit about the stars, but was really still caught in that memory of our first encounter; so I brushed him off saying my goodbyes hurriedly. As I collected my books I could sense that he wanted to say something more. But by then, apart from hating him, I was also burning with the thought that he had successfully spent his time at college, and here I was an utter failure.

7

ARRANGED MARRIAGE AND ME?!

*B*reaking the news to Baba that, far from topping, I had graduated with a second division was heart-wrenching. He didn't speak but the droop of his shoulders said it all. Next few mornings I found him going through matrimonial ads. The postman, too, got into a hyperactive mode, cramming in responses to the ads into our mail box. Bhai was already engaged to be married, so two weddings made economical sense. Ma happily began preparing for both while I was consigned to a bed in the corner of the house with a window, which looked out into the garden to just think, think and think.

A few days later I tried reasoning it out with Baba. I wept and told him of my guilt about being such a lousy daughter who had done incalculable damage to his hopes and dreams and aspirations. We were sitting out in the verandah when I broached the topic with Baba (Ma was luckily out of the house, shopping for vegetables).

'Baba,' I tried, 'I'm really sorry.'

No response. Baba simply continued to stare out at the garden.

'Give me another chance, please. I'll do my MA and

study for the UPSC IAS exam and definitely do you proud,' I continued.

Again no response; I knew that to pursue the topic would be futile. I got up, collecting the tea mugs, when I heard Baba clear his throat.

'You know,' he said, 'you know that you were my child on whom I had invested everything, the one for whom I thought I wouldn't have to go around asking for favours unlike your brother. But you make me feel that all along your mother was right, and I was hopelessly wrong about my faith in you. However, I still want you to go ahead with your dreams, maybe... Wait. The Sinhas are coming tomorrow from Gorakhpur to see you for their son. We'll take a decision after their visit.'

My life has hit the nadir point! Kaun se Sinha? Kahan ke Sinha? And why a Sinha? After my exotic Delhi exposure, the thought of being sent to Gorakhpur married to some Sinha made me tremble.

It's in your moments of decisions that destiny takes a shape. And the Sinha episode turned out to be one such moment. Ek toh they wanted a 'gori' bahu, something coloured like 'moong-ki-daal' or, as my uncharitable mind devilishly muttered, akin to the underbelly of a lizard! After the 'dekho' the next obstacle turned out to be the give-and-take. Baba was opposed to it while the Sinhas were great fans of the dowry system. Short of throwing them out of the house, Baba did everything to speed up their departure from our house. The gate had barely shut on the Sinhas when Baba made the earth-shattering pronouncement that I was to pack my bags and head back for Delhi to seriously devote myself to the IAS studies!

Despite Ma's disapproving sniffles, I was back in Delhi,

of course, this time to stay with Bhai in his tiny little house while IAS beckoned.

The next few months fell into a pattern. I would trundle to the bus stop and take the one-bus-that went-to-the-coaching-centre. If I missed that, the other alternative was to walk. Missing classes, by the way, was no option at all. Bhai would happily and sneakily report that home and this time around there would be no second chances for me!

I made friends with Kavita on the bus. Small, cute and very perky. She got off the bus at the stop after mine and was studying fashion designing. She was fun, well-read and had oodles of male friends who would obligingly give us free rides and also fund our coffee shop bills. She lived close by, had loads of money and knew all the happening places in Delhi.

At the coaching centre, Kiran became a good friend. Since everyone at the centre was a nerd, the choice was restricted and Kiran was less nerdish than the rest. For the third time in my life, I turned nerdish: whenever the spirit flagged, the memories of the Sinhas and the thought of Gorakhpur would restore the balance. As I spent most of my time at the coaching centre and in the library, life was mere books, books, books. The routine was tough and unrelenting. The odd breaks in the canteen would be terribly off-putting. The canteen could be termed a sociologist's delight. Not mine though! People from all over India, all classes of society, everyone in relentless pursuit of a single goal—the IAS. One could encounter the portly Misraji from Jaunpur, having taken his last attempt at the Civil Services exam and working part-time at the centre, the veteran of all the books and the trends in the exams and yet not a qualifier. He would puff away at his cheap cigarettes surrounded by newcomers who were advised to tap him for his 'experience', aka generous guidance the moment they joined the study centre.

Mohanty from Cuttack and a Delhi University education would walk in, rather strut in, to the canteen time to time. He had made it to the top fifty in the last year's IAS list and was the flavour of the month, so to speak.

'Just six hours of study, just six hours are enough,' he'd inform the newcomers taking a break in the canteen. 'You can have my notes from the book store where they've been xeroxed. Just read those and you'll qualify.'

At another table I could spot Subbu. He was from my college and had also done History like me. One attempt had been enough for him. He'd not qualified the exam and was now filling up his apps for a US university. No more the UPSC grind for him. But the mere presence of such types showed the struggle everyone was going through at a personal level to become a professional, to get a job, to eliminate choices and discard ambitions.

Kiran would also be full of dope on the personalities flooding the coaching centre. So-and-so had made it in the first attempt. So-and-so had attempted suicide after failing the last attempt. This one had taken to teaching after repeated failures and married the UPSC topper of some previous batch. She would know whose father was well-connected and would be able to predict their interview marks with astute precision. 'Your father matters, you know,' she'd repeatedly tell me, and my heart would sink more because my father didn't matter in the scheme of things that were UPSC. Apparently, if one was lucky enough to reach the interview stage, book knowledge may not be the only thing one required. The coaching schools said that one's alertness will count as questions like 'how many steps did you walk up to reach here?' or 'what is the colour of the wall behind you?' are thrown at you. Kiran said such mental alertness is not so much required if you have an influential parent with a visible name.

Surprisingly, the teachers were much focused and far superior to the ones I'd encountered at college. The teachers were actually motivated enough to teach! That was a huge revelation. Misraji, of course, had an explanation. In the competitive world of coaching centres, generous pay packages were offered to motivate teachers to get dream results for the institute. Business would start the moment class began and they wouldn't relent an inch; no free periods, no letting off on revision material, no chatting or smart-assing in the class. Boy, this was worse than the Chinese Civil Service exam one had read about in school. You might as well be locked up in a small room and left to slog at studies.

But I was pursuing a goal which I thought would give me freedom and privileges. It'd give Baba a stature and status. Myopically, I dreamt of the days when I would get into a red-beacon adorned car and have hundreds of people salute me. In that hazy dream world, there would also be my partner waiting for me and all would be well with the world.

I knew that my dream was becoming a junoon, when I found Priyanka, my erstwhile best friend from college at the canteen one morning. To say that I was shocked was an understatement.

'I've been looking for you all over. You just dropped out of my life,' Priyanka started tentatively.

'Well, after the way we had parted I didn't think that we should meet.' Also, I accusingly said, 'You didn't tell me that you were a pair with another girl? You both came to Bareilly and misbehaved with my family. It was horrible for me. You put me through such thoughtless trouble.'

Priyanka looked sheepish.

'I know I was wrong. And you know what, it's not really me. I was smarting from my father's treatment. He had slapped me in full public view and had thrown me out of the house after I broke my engagement to a guy of his choice. I was lonely and adrift and that is when this person stepped into my life and one thing led to another.'

After a pause she continued, 'I'd been wanting to meet up with you again and explain things. Hey, I have the tickets for the corporate box in the IPL match for this evening. I know one of the cricketers really well. Why don't we go together and then I'd introduce you to my boyfriend as well?'

Why at all Priyanka had sought me out was suspect. She no longer looked glamorous to me. Actually, she appeared pathetic. Somewhere, the months in that training centre had conditioned me to think that being a butterfly is not all that easy. Either you are a butterfly or you're not. You can't aspire to be part butterfly and part UPSC aspirant. Both are as different from each other as chalk and cheese.

I got rid of her as fast as you could blink an eyelid. She was trouble and I was not longer a fresher from Bareilly seeking glamour. Moreover, was this my last chance from Baba. Kahin yeh bhi gaya to phir (if I let this opportunity slip) I will be a Mrs Sinha from another Bareilly-type town.

8

SLAM!

*T*hat one morning when Kavita did not board the bus, I had a premonition that something was wrong as she was always on the bus in the mornings unless she had somewhere else to go. She had, by then, become an integral part of my life. To escape from Bhai and his fiancée Sweety who'd always want to neck and coo in that barsati, I'd walk over to K's. We'd take her dog out for a walk and dream of the days when we'd be rich and based in London, Tokyo or Paris. We shared a love for Asterix comics and Mills and Boons, which we'd borrow from the local lending library. She'd pay for one day's reading and we'd get the worth of two! Same thing for ice creams. We exchanged make-up, borrowed each other's T-shirts and spent most of our evenings in her bedroom, studying. We swore eternal friendship towards each other.

But obviously something was wrong that morning. Couldn't be viral I thought, considering that I had been with her the evening before.

After classes were over, I made my way to her place. Sarita, the help, opened the door and whispered, 'Didi is in trouble and Madam is blaming you. You go away right now.'

'Kaun hai (Who's there)?'

I heard from inside the house.

It was Aunty and she was at the door before I could make up my mind to run or stay. Aunty was an imposing diamond-ringed matron who had single-handedly brought up her two daughters with an iron fist.

Spotting me she scathingly uttered, 'Oh it's you...'

These three words were enough to make me feel that somehow I needed to run far away from that place. Unfortunately, Aunty's voice was fast and loud.

'You scheming good for nothing creature! I gave you shelter thinking that you were away from your family and needed another home and look how you have stabbed me in the back.'

I could see the neighbours gathering in their balconies for a free soap opera.

'So, all this while, Kavita was running around with that good-for-nothing boy and you were her in cahoots with her?! Instead of studying she was haring off here and there with you as an active accomplice. And here you are, turning up at my door without shame or guilt! How dare you?'

What guilt, what shame? I was really puzzled and also quite terrified at this outburst which was, clearly for me, without any reference or context.

'Don't you dare come in here again!'

SLAM, went the door.

The neighbours wore delighted grins, and considering that Bhai's barsati was a mere two houses away, I was pretty sure that all of this would fast forward its way to him quicker than my reaching home. I turned away. Sarita came running behind to hand over my study books which I must have left in that house in earlier and happier days.

'She's pregnant.'

'Who?'

'Didi. Kavita didi is pregnant.'

'How? How on earth? But I was with her just last evening.'

Sarita giggled.

'She didn't need you to get pregnant! Didn't you know that she was going around with a boy from her firm? And now she is pregnant.'

I couldn't recall Kavita mentioning any particular boy. Moreover, at this point of time I was really keen on knowing how I came into the picture of this development. There was time enough later to feel let down and betrayed that I had been kept in the dark. My immediate concern was why me? And I asked Sarita so.

'Oye, she told Madam that she was with you and staying in your flat, giving you company when your brother was on tour.'

'So she lied,' I spluttered, 'and used my name.'

'Kaun sa romance bina jhoot bole hota hai (Which romance happens without lies)?'

So I was without a friend and also a victim of vilification, with Aunty likely to run a smear campaign against me. I rushed home, found Bhai there without his beloved and told him the entire story. Luckily, he took it well, muttering something about Delhi people and their wealth, and I only got a mild ticking off about not choosing the right friends. It was afterwards that it hit me. I had been friends with someone and not known that she had been sleeping around with someone? All our walks were meaningless and the time spent in careless giggles had been play-acting on K's part. I still couldn't believe it. It was total betrayal. Once again, I had sought a butterfly type of person in my life, someone who was glamorous, without care or concern and who was not focused on a sarkari job, wanting to do things their way. Yet again, my reading of humans turned out to be wrong and off the mark.

It was a disturbance in my tight schedule which I couldn't afford.

9

HORMONAL TWANGS

Well, there was really no time to brood as the UPSC exams were round the corner. Worse still, Sweety too was taking the exam. So we were both competitors as well as collaborators. As the time for the Prelims came closer the tension was unbearable. The canteen appeared as though it would explode if you lit a matchstick. Unshaved boys, or men, unwashed shirts, smoke billowing in the air, smell of sweat, all contributed towards a heady atmosphere. On one table sat two Sikh boys engaged in their books and drinking copious cups of tea.

'The Bindra brothers,' whispered the all-knowing Misraji in my ears. 'Just watch out for them; they are sure-shot to pass this very year. Not like so many others in this room.'

I think I imagined that through his thick glasses he was referring to me when he said this. Another tale doing the rounds was about the examination centre. 'You see how the canteen empties out in the weeks before the exam,' said a worthy. 'It is because several candidates move to smaller towns for the exams. Pucca you stand a better chance if you go to a smaller town.' In such an event I stood no chance having foolishly opted for

Delhi as my centre. Others would mention as to how the best pass percentage came from working people. They were totally experienced in time management and would study methodically and put in exactly the time required.

Stories such as these were definitely off-putting and there really was no one else, apart from Kiran, to turn to in such times. I had blocked myself from the internet and friends from college appeared remote and far away. At home too the solace was limited. Somewhere inside me, panic was building up gradually. Here I was, a 23-year-old friendless, unmarried girl, taking the riskiest exam possible. I felt lonely, very, very lonely.

One afternoon I shifted my base of study to my old university. Fewer disturbances there and the number of UPSC-tale-carrying veterans would be few and far between. As I entered the library I heard someone call out to me in a deep voice. It was Deepak, a very differently turned out Deepak probably back in India taking a break from his studies abroad. A Deepak who looked cool and really hot, and a long suppressed urge rose in me, which I hastily swatted down.

'Hey!' he said. 'Great to see you! Imagine my luck running into you on my very first day back in India.'

'Hi,' I replied nonchalantly. 'You are back?'

'No, just visiting for a while. What a bonus to meet up with you over here. I was vacationing in India and have brought over a friend staying with my family to see the campus.'

The friend turned out to be a total nymphet with blonde hair, a hysterical laugh and a figure to die for. I felt horribly scruffy in my jeans and loose kurta and kholapuri chappals, with hair flying all over the place.

'Chai? How about a cup of tea?' asked Deepak.

It would have been surly of me to say no, and even the best

of Civil Service aspirants take time off for chai and pakoras. So we trundled to the canteen, that very place where I had bumped into him first.

'Oh, how quaint,' said the blonde. 'Is it safe to drink and eat here?'

Deepak merely grinned and we sat down on a rickety table where miraculously tea and samosas appeared looking the same as ever.

We started to chat about Deepak's life abroad while the blonde struggled with the eatables. As was typical, we lapsed into longer Hindi phrases while Deepak updated me about his law programme and how he was branching into criminal law and wanted to go into higher studies. I choose to keep quiet about my Civil Service challenge and what I was doing with my life. No point in discussing what would was a total gamble.

All of a sudden the blonde screeched, 'Look! Look! A fly fell into my tea!'

Deepak was diverted and I got up to go to the library.

'Hang on,' he said, 'why such a rush?'

But rushed I was; there was something I didn't want to tell him at all. Also, there were some hormonal wires twanging in me which I needed to quickly disconnect before anything happened to me.

Of course, the day in the library was a washout. My thoughts went back to Deepak repeatedly and I wondered whether he and the blonde were a twosome. He looked good, really good and yes, a pang of something rose inside me. All round me were couples and lovers, and here I was 23, unkissed and unloved. Nine planets, 195 countries, 800 odd islands, 7 seas, god knows how many people on this planet, and I was Single!

Crash went my studies and gathering the momentum again was a Herculean task. Had my exam centre been at Bareilly, I would've pushed off home. But that option was not available. And damn this Deepak! He always spelt trouble for me. My entire university stay had been warped by his presence, although grudgingly I did feel that he had not done anything at all which I could take offence to. It was just his presence and his silent manner of appearing comfortable with himself. And that blonde. Oh yes, I was really riled by her. I could hear her hysterical laughter in my ears as I forced myself to sleep at night, pillow over my head.

Prelims were two days away when Ma landed up in Delhi. I think she was for once really concerned about me. My centre was in the back of beyond and we planned to commute by an auto. While I took the exam, she opted to sit in the shade of a park close by. It was good that she had come. As I was growing older I felt greater empathy with her and was shifting gears from 'favourite-parent-is-father' to 'favourite-parent-is-mother'.

Mom did a puja type thing before the exam; some dahi and batasha and a tika, which was okay because almost everyone in the centre also came bearing tikas on their forehead. Probably, most of them had been to temples too. Who knows? All that I knew was that the building was a creepy antique sort of a government school. There we were for the biggest exam in our lives, sitting on these rickety desks in a large echoing room, with the sound of the traffic from the street outside clashing its rhythm with the anxious drum-beat of the blood streaming through our brains. My wooden seat was aligned such that it was miles away from the table, which wobbled dangerously. And guess what! One of the Bindra brothers was in my room. For whatever that was worth, I took it as a friendly omen.

The day passed somehow and I was pretty easy in my mind that the exam had gone well. Mom looked nervous as I joined her after the afternoon paper but was relieved that I was confident of my performance. Somehow I had attempted my very first Prelim exam. A year ago it had looked impossible and I was satisfied that I had managed to get into the groove and just do it.

Back in Bareilly, the big discussion was whether or not I should begin my next round of studies for the Mains examination. More so, where should I study? Delhi or Bareilly? The family decided in favour of Delhi. I too thought that the centre had done me good, and I had been able to build a rhythm which would be useful for the next round of studies. Provided that I passed round one, the Prelims exam. So I once again bid farewell to my parents and to Jojo, and moved back to Delhi, joining Bhai at his barsati.

10

PANAUTI! WHO? ME?!

At the centre, the mood for the next round of studies was yet to set in. Anjani, my classmate, came up to me at break time.

'Corbett chalogi? Want to come to Corbett?'

'Corbett?' I asked.

'Haan. Hum sab milke ek group mein jaa rahen hain (we are going there as a group). Thoda break to banta hain na (we do deserve a break)? We are going there as a group, Kiran included.'

Kiran and Anjani were a twosome, so obviously she'd say yes. The rest of the group were a motley crowd of first-timer UPSC types of which Raghu and Vijay were my old college mates, not that I had known them that well while in college. In fact, I tended to avoid them because they were a part of the Deepak–Sudhir gang which never lost an opportunity to rile me with a 'Yaar, tumm to sure shot IAS ho. Kab se pad rahi ho (Buddy, you are a sureshot IAS officer as you have been studying for long)'. My limited encounters with them had been far from pleasant. There had been this all-night rock concert which I attended with some other girls from the hostel, and

Raghu and Vijay had teased me mercilessly thereafter that I had foregone precious study-time to enjoy myself. I had also been the butt of their jokes because of my single status. The joke was that the only affair I could have was with UPSC books.

But Kiran was persuasive and also insistent. 'Chal yaar (Come Buddy.) Chodo in kitabo ko (Leave your books for once.) It's only a three-day trip.'

Raghu's father, who was some hotshot senior officer in the government, had booked us a forest rest house in the interior of the jungle and we were to take the overnight train and return the same way. Over time I got excited at the thought of the trip. The idea of taking three days off from the centre was also quite welcome. Of course, it would mean more cram when I returned but chalta hai (it's okay). Also, everyone around me had done trips of these kind, family holidays to hills and resorts and what not, whereas in our family there was no chance of taking such breaks, let alone enjoying a holiday.

'No way!' shouted Bhai at me. 'Aisa bhi kya break-sheak? (Why do you need a break?) You haven't climbed Mount Everest that you need a holiday. Once the tempo of studies breaks, mind you it will be tough to get back your rhythm. And also,' he said slyly, 'you have enough experience as to how your pendulum can swing from a high to a low as far as your studies go.'

I think that statement clinched it for me and I decided there and then that for me the trip was on. I didn't retort because I needed Bhai on my side so that he wouldn't spill the beans to my hyper father sitting and counting the day to the UPSC Mains in Bareilly!

'I promise, Bhai, you'll find no change in my study pattern. Bas, don't let the parents know, please.'

Actually I could've blackmailed him about his live-in relationship. The parents were hardly aware that their only son was living with his fiancée. But then Bhai is after all a bhai, and in Bareilly all things related to a brother are sacrosanct. He could commit murder, but I can't even kill a fly.

We left the next night. Bhai was in a generous mood; not only did he give me money but he also dropped me off at the station. We had six berths to us and with the train leaving at midnight and reaching Ramnagar at 4:30 a.m., no one was anticipating much sleep. What we didn't anticipate or at least the three of us didn't anticipate was that Kiran and Anjani would gainfully utilize whatever remained of the night on an upper berth. I tried stuffing my ears to block their giggles and Kiran's moaning, but it was tough in the dead of the night. Really, really tough. So that was one night wasted as we alighted at Ramnagar.

Kiran headed for the station dormitory and crashed out on the floor, on her sleeping bag. I sat morosely on the bench outside worrying about the deep jungle where she and Anjani would be discovering more of each other than the environs, which would mean that I would have to spend time with the other boors and heaven knows what ideas they might get seeing these passionate love birds. Frankly, I wanted to return, and return really fast to Delhi.

'Meena! Wake up! The jeep has arrived!'

Obviously I had dozed off on the bench and hadn't been able to work out my escape plan. The love birds meanwhile looked as though they were in paradise. I caught Kiran alone for a fleeting second and hissed at her.

'What on earth are you up to?'

'Up to? Why enjoying life,' was the swift reply. 'Why don't

you also hook up with one of the guys and make most of this time?'

No sense in talking to her. I was caught in a situation which I just didn't know how to handle. We boarded the jeep. It was a squeeze between the five of us and the driver. As we entered the jungle, the guide too joined us, making us seven. I made sure that I was sitting with Kiran on one side and the edge of the jeep on the other. And, of course, Anjani sat on the other side of Kiran. We were too sleepy to appreciate the beauty of the jungle, and soon reached our destination. Stopping the jeep in front of the rest house, the driver pointed out our rooms and advised that we rest and eat while he would be back at two for a deep jungle safari trip.

Luckily, the boys were put up in a dormitory while Kiran and I shared a room. Not so lucky—no one had warned me that there would be no electricity in that place barring for a few hours in the evening! In the oppressive heat I wanted to take off my T-shirt and lie down but was apprehensive of Anjani walking in. A couple of hours later there was a loud banging on our door.

'Come out! Fast! There is a tiger in the water hole. Let's run!' shouted one of the boys.

We ran into the jeep into a tight squeeze as the jeep roared off with me hanging on for my dear life. We were accompanied by other racing jeeps and despite everything, I could sense a thrill. Close to the water hole was a crowd of tourists like us, all on jeeps. Everyone was staring intently into the shrub where apparently a mother tigress lay with her cub. Her tail was visible; the guide informed us in low tones that anytime now she could be expected to emerge, given the heat and her probable desire to have a drink of water.

My view was blocked by the various co-passengers, all of whom were merrily clicking away on their mobiles photographing the scene. We being the last jeep, the crowd ahead was blocking our sight. I didn't want to miss seeing my very first tiger and was turning and twisting and arching my neck to focus on its tail.

'Where is she?' I finally asked.

'Husshh,' was the sharp response from the collective crowd. 'Keep quiet else she'll go away.'

'Get down, Raghu,' I said to my co-passenger who was blocking my view. As he didn't react, I repeated the request a little louder. Just then the tigress walked into the deep and disappeared altogether.

'Awwww!' Came a collective cry. 'Who the hell spoke so loudly? See, the tigress has gone into the deep. Kya yaar abhi tak to awesome sighting hone ka chance tha.'

Lots of accusatory glances came in my direction and I was crowned the 'panauti' of my group; a bad omen and a very unlucky person. I heard Raghu tell the others, 'Arre, agli trip mein esse mat bulana, woh panauti hai (Don't invite her on the next trip, she is bad luck).'

Somehow we passed the remaining time on the safari giving desultory glances to monkeys and peacocks and deer. At the rest house, unable to bear the mere fact that not only had I been abandoned by my friend but was also the butt of ridicule, I headed straight for the room. As night set in, I stepped out and sat under the lone peepul tree in the rest house compound, watching the glowworms in the dark against the incessant cries of peacocks.

'I felt really bad for you out there,' suddenly someone uttered. It was Vijay. 'Raghu had no business speaking the way he did.'

I think I must've been looking for sympathy, otherwise there was no rational explanation for me giving even half an ear to this character. So I sniffed. Not a crying sniff but a sniff that can be interpreted that way. Vijay sat down next to me and started giving me a lowdown on Raghu and the general facts surrounding his life and as to how he, Vijay, had to play second fiddle to a more powerful, more influential and more-everything-than-him Raghu. If I weren't so absorbed in self-pity I would've thought that he was actually bitching, and if there was one golden rule in our Bareilly household, it is that 'thou shall not carry tales about another.' How else was Bhai so comfortable that his cozy situation with the fiancée would remain a secret? But to err is human, and I let Vijay continue, taking my silence as tacit acceptance of the truckloads of criticism of Raghu.

Something ran down my back. I didn't react thinking that it may be a small beetle or an insect. Meanwhile, Vijay slithered closer. This time I saw it! Despite the darkness, I saw it! It was Vijay's finger running down my back!

'Ohji, hello hello! What on earth do you think you are doing?' I screamed.

'Nothing. Nnnnothing... just.'

'Just what, heh?' I asked belligerently.

Hearing me shout, Raghu and others came to the tree.

Seeing them, Vijay did a 360-degree volte-face, a regular turnaround and drawled, 'Yaar guys, Meena had called out to me to sit with her until dinner was served. I don't know what happened. All of a sudden she went into these loud screams.'

What an utter creep!

I immediately confronted him.

'Didn't you touch me? Run a finger down my back?'

'Finger? Me? Down your back? Not in a million years,' was the response pat and smooth and coated in lies. Vijay guffawed.

Kiran stepped in to ask, 'Look, Vijay, I know Meena, she doesn't make up stories. Come out with the truth. Please.'

Before anyone else could say anything, Raghu aggressively said, 'Chodo yaar, Meena ki baat ka kya bharosa (Leave it guys, who on earth trusts this girl)? Come Vijay, let's go for dinner.'

I was rooted to the ground, shell shocked. What exactly did Mr Great-shakes-Raghu mean when he said that my word can't be trusted? Me? I am the most trustworthy, honest, clear-hearted person, and that's the way I have been brought up by Baba. This time I really sniffed and moved to my room holding back tears. Kiran followed me.

'Go away!' I sharply told her. 'If it weren't for you and that Anjani making out all the time, this wouldn't have happened.'

Looking distinctly sheepish, Kiran decided to keep quiet. A little later, we heard a knock at the door. Anjani came in with a plateful of food. I turned my face to the wall so that he'd leave, which he did fast and quick but Kiran hung on.

'Kuch kha le, yaar,' she tried to cajole. 'Eat something please. I am sorry for everything turning out the way it has.'

No reaction from me. One thing Baba had taught us is to keep our pride intact. So what if this friendship went out of the window. I'd been fooled into taking a trip with her and been labelled a 'panauti' and a liar. A little later I heard her crying and sniffling as she started off with her sob story about how her parents in Kerala had fixed her marriage with a cashew nut king based in Dubai, and how this was her last chance to spend this glorious time with Anjani, her true and only love, the memories of whom would last her a lifetime of a loveless and lonely marriage.

All of this was way too much for me and the memory of Baba suddenly made me realize my main mission in life.

'If you are getting married, then what happens to your IAS aspirations?' I asked Kiran. 'The exam is just three months away, so how can you get married?'

She looked as though I'd gone mad. Here she was telling me of her life-shattering problems while my reaction was limited to the Civil Services exam. Controlling her thoughts, which may have been murderous, she sharply reacted, 'Forget the IAS. That was an excuse to be around in Delhi and away from my parents. Falling in love with Anjani was a bonus.'

My thoughts turned topsy-turvy as everything that I had considered as common between us turned out to be a mirage. There was nothing more to be said. She left and it was over. Finito.

Next morning, I found that the group planned to return for Delhi sooner than planned, which suited me just as well. It was perhaps the longest journey for all of us, taken in absolute silence. All barring Raghu who, apart from making a snide remark about how much trouble his father had taken to organize the programme, which we had hastily and prematurely terminated, comfortably snored his way through.

11

MEET VENKAT REDDY

I trundled up to the barsati, sleep deprived and totally dazed by the events of the past few days. Sweety, clad in a nighty, was brewing tea while Bhai was somewhere inside.

'Back early, I say,' she said, 'what happened?'

'Nothing. The trip was no fun and too rough to be a real break,' I said.

Giving me a sly look and a cup of tea Sweety asked, 'Kuch boy shoy ka scene nahi bana? No luck with the boys? I thought you'd finally made up your mind to get into a relationship. Waise bhi, I was telling your brother that two girls and three boys never ever go on such a trip unless, of course, some wires are twanging between them.'

Really, I don't know what Bhai saw in that girl, but my respect went up for him if he hadn't created a fuss about this trip despite his dear and beloved trying to attribute a motive to an otherwise innocent outing. I sipped the tea wondering how to get my act together and shake off that sense of utter hopelessness that seemed to have seeped into every micro-centimetre of my being. The more immediate problem was how to pass the day. It was a Sunday and with Sweety parading around in the nighty, I was pretty sure that the two of them had plans for the day where my presence made me a kebab-mein-haddi; I'd be a definite fly in the soup if I hung around at home. Dying for sleep and now feeling even more unwanted than ever, I moved to the tiny bathroom to bathe and then head off for the university library, which was mercifully open on Sundays.

The long bus ride was therapeutic. The library became my refuge that morning, but there was little motivation to study, and I spent the entire day there alternately doodling and moping. What do I do with myself now? I was obviously a misfit who was heading for disaster by taking the Civil Services exam in which there was little chance for me to qualify. Given the state of affairs, the alternative was to marry someone in Gorakhpur or Meerut or some such place—such a gruesome thought.

Stepping out of the library I decided to call Baba at the spur of the moment.

'Baba,' I said querulously, my voice choked.

'What happened, Beta?'

'I can't do this anymore, Baba. Can I come home and then we can talk over other options?'

'Arre bachche. Kyon ghabra rahi ho? (Baby, why are you worrying so much)? After all, this exam is a very tough one and ups and downs are a part of it. Go take a break and then you'll feel better. After all, studying 11–12 hours a day can be mentally tiring, and your brother was telling me how you had been burning the midnight oil these last few days.'

Three cheers for Bhai but what to do? I needed someone, anyone, to be with me emotionally, hold my hand through this mess; Baba was on his own wavelength. He continued telling me about his surgeon friend's son who had qualified the exam last year and who was now on his Bharat Darshan, a trip to familiarize young bureaucrats with India. He concluded our conversation heartily by telling me that soon I would be in the IAS training academy in Mussoorie, and that such moments of nervousness would be a thing of the past.

Next morning I headed for the institute. Pretty convinced that Mr Raghu and his dear friend Vijay would sully the institute with their own version of the trip, I decided to take the shit head on. Misraji was already at a table chatting with someone; he waved me over.

'Come, come. Meet Venkat Reddy,' he said. Venkat was a thin, tall, good lookingish person wearing a pale blue shirt and sporting aviators. He and Misraji made a strange twosome, but I joined them in any case.

'Hi!' I said morosely.

'Arree! Hi se nahi banega (Just hi won't suffice),' said Misraji. 'Venkat has been allotted UP. Good state. All UP IAS officers do well. Cabinet secretaries and all that.'

Really? Misraji should write a fact book on the IAS, so obsessed is he with the service, and so ready that he is with all his data on IAS types.

Venkat was a man of few words and just as well, since it seemed he had done little in his life but study. First IIT (Indian Institute of Technology) Delhi, followed by this exam and not to forget that he had also cracked the CAT and would've joined IIM (Indian Institute of Management) had he not got into the IAS. Wow! What a cat! And yes, what a nerd.

'How was your trip to Corbett?' asked Misraji.

'Okay.'

'Tiger dekha? Did you get to spot a tiger?'

'Kind of,' I responded, and just to change the topic. I launched off onto some book I had read on tigers. In my convoluted thinking I presumed that Venkat probably never read books, busy as he had been studying his entire life. Also, I must confess that us Humanities type have a deep feeling of pity for the Science passouts, who seem to do little else apart from wasting their childhood and young adulthood poring over textbooks.

Venkat surprised me by not only matching me with the details of the book, but he actually beat me with some reference from it, which I seem to have missed. Misraji meanwhile yawned through the entire discussion. He finally drifted off, bored and disappointed that the conversation had veered away from the Civil Services exam. I too left shortly for my next class while other students came over to greet Venkat.

The Sociology teacher droned on about Sanskritization and Westernization, concepts which seemed so very critical to Indian society. Bored, tired and totally confused I jotted down ten reasons for my current state:

Reason One: Baba's desire that I take the Civil Services examination.

Reason Two: Baba felt that the car with the flashing red beacon in which I would travel once I became an officer would be a huge retribution to the sorrows that life had doled out to him.

Reason Three: Baba felt that I shouldn't get married for dowry.

Reason Four: Hello?! Reason four? Come again? There is no Reason Four.

Everything seemed to centre on Baba this and Baba that, as if my own free will had no role to play in my life choices. Honestly, it seemed to me that my own decision-making options were zero. Non-existent.

So, obviously, the next issue which arose was what would I do if I had to make a choice for myself? Option One: Hello?! Option Two: Blank. No, Maybe I'd look around for a rich man who would take care of my family's financial problems and carry with him a status that would soothe Baba's aspirations.

That's all? I asked myself. Apparently so. Which meant that at twenty-three my entire life's aspirations were limited to somehow getting hooked onto a man who could sort out Baba's problems! Boy!

There was no point in proceeding with those thoughts and I succumbed to the Sociology teacher.

12

FOCUS, FOCUS, FOCUS!

So passed the summer months and before I knew it, the nail biting days close to the date when the Prelims results would be declared arrived. Mom told me that Baba would be in the puja room 24x7. For the students, there was little solace. While we were preparing for the next hurdle, the Mains later in the year around end October, our fate in the Prelims was uncertain.

Meanwhile Venkat came pretty frequently to the institute as he was posted close by in Ghaziabad. I would end up joining the group chatting with him about his experiences. Well, he was one of those rare types who had hit the jackpot by qualifying in his first attempt at the exam. So, I guess he enjoyed some sort of a cult status.

On the social front, my choices were now limited. Kiran had moved back to Kerala after a huge scene with her family when they found out about Anjani. She got married too; not that I got invited. I was able to avoid Vijay. Raghu dropped out, and I learnt later that he had developed cold feet about the Civil Services exam and his father had fixed him up in some fancy American university, fully paid. No wonder everyone and their kith and kin want to become a civil servant; it seems to open up doors to money, influence and power.

'Bindra bhi drop kar gaya (Bindra has dropped out as well),' said Misraji one day dramatically. 'You won't be seeing junior Bindra any more over here, he has dropped out.'

Now, in the civil servant aspirant's lexicon, dropout is akin to announcing that someone is threatened with a life shattering disease. One only dropped out if one got married (for girls), or one fell ill, or if one were lily-livered (a la Raghu) or, well, if lady luck smiled on one and one got another job. For a civil servant aspirant that other job had to be of similar status (read officer type) and not something chota sa, something lower. But Bindra had not struck a lottery. He just moved on to taking an assistant inspector's job in the customs department. No doubt also a government job, but it was definitely notches below in status. According to Misraji, this was done because, on his third attempt at the exam, Bindra felt that things continue to be uncertain. He was nervous and perhaps grabbed at the opportunity available.

'Ghabra gaya ladka (the boy got scared),' said Misraji.

I wondered about this. If I were taking other government exams like Bindra, would I too have opted out at the first available opportunity? Can't say really because Baba had insisted that I take the Civil Services exam only. And also, I wondered about Misraji, permanently a resident of the Coaching Institute, now in his 30s, portly, tight-clothed, all-knowing and paan-chewing, taking vicarious pleasure from the success and failure of others in this tortuous exam. He had reinvented his ego instead of himself. He undertook a journey, didn't reach the destination but failed to start another one. In the end what matters is how well one has lived one's life, not how many successes one has achieved. As Priyanka once told me, if a king has painful piles, what is the use of a diamond-studded golden throne?

'Don't walk down that path,' cautioned Venkat, as though he read my thoughts about Misraji.

'There is no success or failure. In this exam it's plain hard work and some luck. In fact, it is the most opaque exam in India and you end up trusting the process blindly. There may be lacunae in the way examinations are held but there is never corruption involved in the recruitment process. You can trust it. There are close to 5 lakh aspirants each year, though I understand some 9 lakh have applied this year, of which around 3 lakh finally take the Prelims. Some 10,000 to 20,000 qualify for the Mains, and of these around 2,000–2,500 are called for the interview to fill up around 800–1,000 slots. It's really a combination of luck and hard work; sheer unadulterated chance.'

'I wasn't really...,' I sputtered back at Venkat, as if justifying my thoughts about Misraji.

'He is a good-hearted soul and he will now move full-time to the faculty of this institute and eventually make a career in either journalism or law. Guys like Misraji are around in plentiful and they mess up their lives forever thinking of what could've been had they only met with success. But destiny had other things in store for them.'

I listened wide-eyed. There was more to him than all that degrees. He continued in the same vein, 'That is why it is critical to give your hundred per cent to this phase in your life. There are many distractions and conflicting thoughts to divert you, but it has to be focus, focus, focus all the way.'

I got the uncomfortable feeling that Venkat had moved

beyond Misraji and was now trying to tell me something. So, I sort of squirmed and edged closer to the exit mudra on my chair. But you can't leave a friendly face and that too an IAS officer's, like you could to others, while he is mid-stream in some sort of a discourse. The nerd seemed to have a deeper side to him, I thought.

'You can crack it without pain provided you set daily goals for yourself. Take me for instance, I knew that I could move on to a better paid environment even if I didn't qualify for this exam, but I wanted to do it for myself, which I did. Though lakhs of aspirants apply and write this exam, the real competition is between only 2,000–3,000 serious aspirants. Those who study systematically and consistently get into service. If you do the same, you will be one among them. Don't have fears even before you start. Remember to make the process fun, enjoy reading, love what you do and do everything to please yourself. Not for your parent or sibling or society.'

Despite the dark aviators, I could see his pin-pointed gaze running through me laser sharp. Had he figured that I was hardly interested in the exam and that it was my father's mission I was executing?

13

ME, THE SANYASIN

Oh well, life moved on to July and before one could blink, it was August and result time. The centre also was a bit nervy because its raison d'être depended upon the performance of the students. According to Misraji, in the pre-historic days of the Civil Services exam, one had to line up in UPSC itself to get to know one's results. A jostling crowd would gather there, armed with roll numbers.

'Waise toh seeing the result with your own eyes is not of a problem but you know, it is better to be sure than sorry,' said Mr Final Word on the Civil Services exam.

The chaiwalla had his own story. There was an erstwhile student of this institute, who had mistakenly treated everyone to chaat on the lane leading up to the UPSC gate without re-confirming his roll number. Dumb of him, no doubt, but in the sensitive stage that I was, any story like this was like a Ramsay Brothers' horror story.

Baba had my roll number, so I guess we'd all connect online and get to know the result. I let him do the needful and occupied myself reading a Mills & Boon when the results were due. From the ecstatic heaving and loud sobs at the end of Baba's call I knew that I was through the first hurdle. Yes! I had cleared the Prelims. I now belonged to Venkat's 10,000 group who would take the Mains in a couple of months. Unfortunately though, Sweety had not qualified, and to her credit she failed to appear hassled about it.

Meanwhile, Venkat had become a menace. Just because I had sat once or twice with him in the canteen and listened to his fundas did not mean that he could take liberties and attribute a deeper motive to our relationship. I received a hysterical call from Ma one afternoon. And mind you, Ma is never hysterical.

'Are you having an affair?'

'Me?'

'Your brother called about some South Indian who called him up to talk about you.'

'Talk what?'

'Well…' said Ma and shut up. She didn't know what Venkat dear had called up Bhai for. But that set me thinking. When Ma called I was in the barsati and Bhai was sitting pretty much in there. Why had he not mentioned the call to me and instead called our parents? I wasted an entire afternoon of studies which, like, means a lot when the Mains are just a skip and jump away.

Restless, I finally confronted Bhai, a gentle sort of confrontation, not very aggressive.

'Bhai, Ma said that Venkat called you. I didn't know that you knew him.'

'I don't.'

'Then why did he call? Like, what did he talk about to you?'

'Some work or the other. Oh! I remember, he wanted a affidavit prepared.'

What an absolutely weak response?! It took the cake but

also shut me up. Venkat couldn't possibly want Bhai to prepare an affidavit for him! He had like tonnes of minions hanging around him in Ghaziabad to do that. Well, I had to satisfy myself with that and get done with mugging up vague facts on Geography for the General Studies paper.

Meanwhile, as the days moved towards the big exam, dear Venkat stopped coming to the institute, which was just as well because finally I'd got my rhythm right. I'd also moved base partly to these so-called libraries where one could pay an hourly rate and find a seat to study in air-conditioned comfort. These were not real libraries, just huge study rooms which are quite popular with UPSC types because they are safe and cool and quiet and all students there share the common goal and speak the common language.

Actually, you can make out an UPSC type at this stage from a distance. Partly unwashed, somewhat unkempt and wholly frenzied. No time even to listen to Misraji. He too had gone bonkers as though he was attempting to the take the exam himself, yet again. The institute had informed that in order to save time we needn't read the newspapers ourselves. Misraji would go through the lot, identify the important clippings and send these to us. We were informed that managing time during the preparation is the most important aspect in preparing for this examination. Good to hear about the papers, I for one always opened up Page 3 first and got lost in the world of Lady Gaga and other gossip before moving on to the boring but more relevant world of real news.

So there I was. No TV. No radio. No internet. And now, no newspaper. Throw in the fact that rare was the day when water and electricity wasn't an issue in that barsati, and I could be renamed a sanyasin!

14

HOME!

Then came the Mains. I'd stuck a huge post-it on the wall behind my study table to motivate me. It read:

Success is 1% luck and 99% perspiration.

So it was. The atmosphere was so charged that ions were crackling. But somehow, I got through the papers, the Optionals, the Language, the Subject papers, et al.! Phew, I heaved a sigh of relief. As my subjects were Humanities, I couldn't estimate my actual performance in the subjects and was completely disheartened by the General Studies paper, which made one feel like an illiterate. The institute's preparations were nowhere close to the real world of the General Studies paper. No great marks waiting for me there, I concluded.

Once the papers were over, I decided to push off to Bareilly the very next day. Bhai came to drop me off at the station. Ever since his lady love had abandoned her shot at the exams, he had been giving me his undivided attention, including doing the exam centre duty. Also, with his wedding scheduled to take place within the next few weeks, he had actually become a nicer person. At the station he cryptically uttered, 'Your pal Venkat had called me to wish you luck.'

That blasted Venkat! Why couldn't he have called me?

'Probably didn't want to disturb you,' said Bhai, reading my thoughts. Actually Bhai was appearing conspiratorial and smirking and I almost thought I saw him wink at me.

What was the point of reacting to this? So I kept quiet and by and large chose to be that way until I boarded the train armed with a *Femina* (Yes! What luxury and bliss to be able to read one!) and a bottle of mineral water. But truthfully, I couldn't concentrate on reading at all. I kept on fuming at Venkat. That silly fellow was ruining my peaceful family equilibrium by calling up Bhai at periodic intervals to check on me. I wouldn't have shared that table with him in the institute nor gone to Bareilly apprehensive that my darling brother had informed my parents about Venkat's phone calls; there would be lots and lots of putting two and two together to arrive at conclusions, which I didn't want to think of.

Baba was there to receive me at the station. There was a gush of joy in my heart as I saw him standing on the platform looking the same in his loose trousers and bush-shirt. In the car I discovered to my joy that he had bought me my favourite chola bhaturas! Jojo bounced all over nearly knocking me down as I hugged Ma. I surveyed the garden, checked out the plants and the changes in the little patch and generally felt happy. It was a blissful feeling to know that I could take a wee bit of a break until the interview call came, that is, if it came at all. The four of us, including Jojo, sat down for tea. Tea was always an important ritual in our household; something I had never really relished until this time. Just the warmth and the routine of sitting down amongst love was a therapeutic feeling. We discussed Bhai's wedding arrangements and the list of invitees and such like.

As Ma cleared up, I moved to Baba's little clinic to check out the Bareilly newspapers. Lo and behold, the Great Mr Venkat's name hit my eyes. He'd been transferred to Bareilly and that was news to me! I just hoped that our paths would not cross; I was determined to give this guy a solid piece of my mind.

'Meena,' I heard Ma shout out, 'we have to attend the Rastogis' daughter's wedding reception at the Bareilly Club tonight. Why don't you also come along?'

Now that was a definite change in attitude. My parents were now willing to treat me as a grown-up, seeking my consent to attend a tacky function. Earlier I'd would have been dragged to it, kicking and screaming, with Ma insisting that she'd rather we all eat there than her having to cook a meal just for me if I stayed back.

With my new found sense of maturity after the rigour of isolation and study I decided to accompany them. In any case, I loved going to the Bareilly Club right from early childhood. Started by the British, Bareilly Club is the oldest and the most coveted club of Bareilly. The atmosphere there is family-oriented and it is simply gorgeous. I was sure to meet some of my old friends no doubt married and with kids now, but it'd be good to meet them in any case.

As I walked in with my parents, I could spot familiar faces in the crowd and lo and behold, I met my old friend Sunita. We hugged in ecstatic delight, even though our parting years ago had been less than cordial. I was introduced to her pot-bellied businessman husband who, on one hand, sported the jazziest watch I'd seen any human wear. On the same hand he carried an overflowing glass of whiskey. Frankly, I was secretly relieved that I'd not headed in the direction of marriage after school like Sunita and others; I really needed to be grateful to Baba who actually nursed a deeper ambition for me than I had for myself.

We were joined by a few other girls from my school, all of whom looked decidedly more glamorous than I could recall. Definitely Bareilly had become hip! They were dressed to kill, one of them even sporting a tight black dress with a lot of leg show. Bareilly had apparently hit glamour big time after Priyanka Chopra made it big in Bollywood. The girls were at pains to inform me that the city now hosted a number of fashion shows too. Oh well. The conversation then moved on to other actresses who came from Bareilly and the films shot in the city. Luckily, the list was short because my mind was now far, far away. If you ask me, at that point I would willingly be back at the institute listening to Misraji warble on and on about IAS officers and the exam than listen to the crap these girls seemed to be talking.

I wandered off when the ladies decided to list out the songs with Bareilly featuring in them. From '*Jhumka Bareilly waala kaanon mein aisa daala*' to '*New Delhi mein Bareilly Jaisa Saiyaan*', they were so hugely jingoistic about the city that it was jarring my nerves. As if the entire effort was to prove to me that the city which I had left for Delhi was a little paradise in itself.

'What a surprise?!'

I jerked around to see Venkat standing there with that familiar look, and man, was I not happy to see someone who was not ranting and raving about the joys of living in Bareilly. Which meant that my reaction to him was more enthusiastic than it should have been. I totally forgot that I was sore with him over those calls to Bhai.

'Hey!' I said. 'Great to see you!'

'Didn't know that you were visiting this place,' said Venkat.

If I had not been so put off by the Bareilly girls, I'd have reacted by asking him what made him think that I needed to tell him of my whereabouts.

Well, we continued to chat for a bit about the Mains and he asked some very serious questions, nodding knowingly and approvingly, which ended up in me telling him more and more. So much so that thirty minutes or so later, Sunita's husband came looking for me. Ma and Sunita had got frantic about my absence from the reception and had put him to the task of searching me out. He was thrilled to be introduced to Venkat, being an IAS officer and all that, and insisted that he should also join in the reception party as though he were the host. I mildly protested because I'd seen the host standing at the dinner table counting the plates, and if Venkat ate then it would be one plate more to be paid for. But Mr Sunita bulldozed Venkat, who was haplessly dragged into the post-wedding chaos of aunties and uncles and school friends and what not. Of course, he got the royal treatment from everyone and was eventually swallowed up in a sea of men.

My erstwhile schoolmates once again collected around me, tittering away. They were really irritating! Venkat's official position had made him an object of interest and somehow they all wanted me to bring him over for dinners and teas and lunches to their homes.

Shaking them off, I pleaded a headache and requested Baba that we leave, which we thankfully did.

15

WHAT ABOUT VENKAT?

I stretched myself awake the next morning, Jojo curled at my toes, birds chirped in the rose bushes outside. It was lovely being home, in the comfort of my bed. As I sauntered to the kitchen, I could sense that something was the matter. Regardless, I cheerfully greeted my parents with a 'Morning! Good to be home!' And then, noticing Baba was still at home and not at work, I asked, 'What's up Baba? You haven't left as yet for work?'

'Humph,' was his short response, while all of a sudden the clatter of dishes in the sink became louder. All signals pointed to tension. I chose to ignore it and settled down with the paper, ever conscious that perhaps the third stage of the exam, i.e., the interview, awaited me, and that I needed to read the papers to keep abreast of news, etc.

'Do you have something to tell us?' Baba shot at me.

I peered bemusedly at him, from the side of the paper. Obviously, a response was expected. Perhaps there was something that sneak of my brother had tattled about me. Maybe about money or that I hadn't studied enough or some such stuff. But I chose to play it cautiously.

'Tell you what?'

'Humph,' went Baba again and looked at Ma.

'You go to the hospital, and I'll handle it,' Ma spoke.

Hello?! Handle what? And that's exactly what I asked her.

'What's the matter, Ma? What has Bhai told you about me?'

Ma gave me a strange look and said, 'It's nothing to do with your brother.'

'Then? What's this heavy duty stuff about, Ma?'

'That Venkat…'

'Venkat? What about him?'

Oh dear! It hit me that not only my family, but by now, half of Bareilly was building up stories about Venkat and me being a couple, the mere thought of which was gruesome. I know that I've not been particularly stable in my friendships and have perhaps been more of a rolling stone, and that is exactly why Venkat was not a friend, or worse still, someone I would be in a relationship with. But before I could protest and clear matters, some pal from Ma's kitty group called up, and from the look on Ma's face and her terse responses, I could fathom that the conversation was about the evening at the club last night.

So, I escaped to the garden. My options were few and unpractical. Mostly, I wanted to throw my cup of tea at Venkat, and also perhaps knock him out cold with Bhai's old cricket bat. Stupid fellow! He had become my self-appointed mentor and, of all the things, had managed to spoil the one break that I was taking with my parents, after months, by getting posted in Bareilly of all the places. Well, there was a simple solution to the whole thing. I'll not take his calls and avoid places where we could meet, such as the Bareilly Club, and mainly hang around the house and be incommunicado. Rumours really spread fast in small towns.

But things aren't all that simple. A week passed with this silence, both between my parents and me on this issue, and between Venkat and me, and all I did was shop and read up for the interview. Venkat though is irrepressible.

One evening the doorbell rang and there Venkat was in our house. Jojo leapt up at him barking loudly which, I was thrilled to note, unnerved him totally. Hopefully, if Jojo didn't like Venkat then the visit would be short, I thought.

'What are you doing here?' I came straight to the point.

'Kaun hain?' Ma asked, entering the room.

On seeing Venkat, an all-knowing look came on her face. I wanted to shout out loud, No! No! No! This is not what you are imagining.

'Arre! Andar aao Beta. Come in. Come in. Stop it Jojo!' She said all in one breath and dragged Jojo away to lock him up.

'You don't look happy to see me.'

'Oh no! Nothing like that,' I responded, but my tone was lacklustre and pretty unenthusiastic. 'Come in.'

'I was in the neighbourhood and thought I'd drop by and check out how things were with you.'

'You'll have water?' was my response, and I trotted off into the kitchen to fetch him a glass.

Hopefully when he'll have to sit alone in our drawing room with its peeling walls and single tubelight, he'd feel unwelcome and hasten his departure from my house. But just then Baba came in. One thing led to another, and before I knew Venkat was seated at the dining table sharing our dinner and also feeding Jojo scraps. Baba was impressed by his methodical approach to the Civil Services exam, and got totally energized when Venkat started off on how I could prepare for the interview. That somehow clinched matters. Now I pretty much expected that our dining table would turn into the canteen table. Was he not a lonely type?! I mean, I too am pretty low on the friends scene, but like hanging around the canteen and driving down all the way from Ghaziabad just to hang out there and now coming home like this. Didn't he have anything else to do? Say a hobby or some friends or anything?

So, Venkat became part and parcel of our household, even volunteering for Bhai's shaadi preparations, and ever so often loaning his lal-batti car to Ma when she needed to visit the more crowded shopping areas. I strictly kept the conversation limited to the interview preparations but that was not wholly possible. When Bua, my father's sister, came over in the week before the wedding, she would clear her throat each time she saw me and speak of so and so's daughter-in-law who gave half the Civil Services exam midway between getting married, and yet qualifying. Another time it was about some other character who gave the exam while pregnant and yet qualifying. I'm not dumb, but unless confronted with a direct question on the relationship status between Venkat and me, I chose silence. Luckily Baba came to my rescue, and shortly after, this type of talk was abandoned.

16

MR GOODY TWO-SHOES

The wedding was good fun. I'd actually grown fond of my sister-in-law and participated vigorously in all the festivities. I'd also decided to move out of the barsati, when back in Delhi, and to shack up with other girls in a PG. It would be the best wedding present I'd give to the newlyweds. Baba would need some convincing but that hurdle could be crossed once the wedding was over.

Mr Goody Two-shoes Venkat came for the reception. After greeting the newlyweds he made his way towards me, and half of the Bareilly crowd looked on with eagerness and in anticipation.

'You look nice,' he said.

'Make-up and glamourous clothes,' I said.

'Yes. But you have chosen a good colour for your dress. You know some people mess up with their colour choices and then look ghastly. Or add too much bling and look like chandeliers.'

'Gosh! I hope you are not going to give gyan about this also? Venkat, you are incorrigible! You seem to have a view on everything!'

Did I sense that he looked a bit hurt at that? A few cursory words later he made off and I saw him leave early without taking dinner. Meanwhile, the dance floor was ablaze with all age groups shaking a leg or two. Soon Bhai and his wife dreamily danced to my all-time favourite song *I Want to Break Free* by Queen. Yes, I felt a bit jealous and lonely seeing them moon over each other. But I shook off the thought. Time enough for that later on.

17

GO, FIGHT, WIN!

*W*inding up after the wedding took a bit. There were bills to be paid, relatives to be dropped off at the station and bus stand, material and bedding borrowed or hired to be returned. Since Bhai had pushed off for his honeymoon, I thought I should be around to help my parents. Of course, I wish I too had left for Delhi immediately because when I left Bua at the bus stop for her ride back home she lost no opportunity in telling me that my dark-skinned intellectual-looking boyfriend was a good choice on my part. She also said that him being an IAS was a bonus, and that I had erred by not getting married to him along with Bhai; that would have saved my parents the cost of another wedding.

Which reminded me, the great Shri Venkat had mysteriously disappeared and not been seen in our house since the evening of the reception. Yes, I admit that I did wonder if it was the result of our last encounter. And yes, when ten days passed, I did get a bit concerned and thought of sending him an SMS, or perhaps go across and visit him in his office.

Sunita called one evening to invite me to attend a World Cup Football party at her place. It was a theme party and the men had to sport the colours of their favourite football teams. The girls had to come geared up as fancy cheerleaders! Really, Bareilly had undergone a solid makeover! I asked her about what to wear. Sunita helpfully advised that I could wear a short skirt and a T-shirt, carry pom-poms, sport a bow and a flag of my favourite team.

Like hell I'd do so! My limited knowledge of football was what I had studied for the Civil Services exam and to cheer for anyone with that bit of information was to live with the uncomfortable thought that I needed to study harder for my likely interview call. But I still went for the party. A quick Google search revealed that cheerleaders can also wear tracks and tees, which is what I did, and landed up at Sunita's grand mansion, spread over four stories with a swimming pool thrown it to complete the I-have-arrived look.

Mr Sunita greeted me warmly with a 'Hello! Hello! Look who is here?' at the entrance, though he did look taken aback at my version of a cheerleader's attire. We exchanged a few pleasantries; I complimented him on his Manchester City outfit and moved towards the crowd where almost the first person I spotted was Venkat clad in trousers and a white shirt. If anything, he was more unsuitably attired for the do than me. Then, he gave me a lovely grin, a non-Venkatish grin which made him appear more charming and relaxed than I had ever seen him look. I greeted him politely.

'Wow! You are dressed as the manager of a football team!' gushed Sunita at Venkat, as she rushed towards us.

She did look a sight with her short pink skirt, a cheerleader pink bow and pom-poms tied around her wrists.

'Meenaaaa!' she then admonished, 'Couldn't you have dressed more to the party theme? Look at you? You look as if you are stepping out for a walk or hitting the bed.' And, having said her itsy-bitsy nasty bit, she moved on gesturing us to enjoy ourselves.

I was crestfallen. But before I could retreat into a corner and plan a speedy escape in my inept attire, Venkat surprised me by grinning more and offering a few consoling words.

'Just wait till you become an officer and everything you do will be acceptable. See how I have been converted into a football team manager, when I am merely wearing my normal office clothes. So, I can't be wrong. I am who I am, whereas you can't be because you aren't anyone as yet.'

Well, Venkat seemed to have a good idea about Bareilly's high society. One only mattered if one was an officer. So, Venkat was here because he was an officer and I was here either because I was a potential officer or because I knew Venkat.

I moved towards to a group of some schoolmates and their better-halves and listened to one of the men go on and on about how only Vitamin M (money) mattered in India today. Despite knowing my honest aspirations of becoming an IAS officer he went on to state that nothing mattered except bribes; that's how he become the proud owner of a huge business of educational institutes.

And so the party went on. My mind was definitely prompting me to leave; somewhere, the thought that I had felt so happy to see Venkat was killing me. I was also guilty that I had not made amends with him regarding my behaviour at Bhai's wedding reception. But there was no opportunity to do so; Venkat seemed to be enjoying himself being at the centre of a group of whiskey guzzling men, while he himself sipped on nariyal pani or some such.

The crowd got bigger and very inebriated; the mood of

bonhomie and joie-de-vivre was all over. Much as I wanted to escape, with Mr Sunita still planted at the gate welcoming late comers, that option wasn't available. So I stood, marvelling yet again at my erstwhile school friends who were dressed to the nines, and who made cute cheer leaders to their pot-bellied T-shirt clad husbands. There were several kids running all over, which indicated that booze and theme parties and skimpily-clad mammas were an accepted deal for the Bareilly tots.

'Now, it's time for games!' I heard Sunita shout, megaphone in hand. 'We'll be in two groups and play antakshari, and each time someone sings well, the girls will cheer and wave their pom-poms!'

Someone handed me a printed copy of the cheerleader's slogan which read:

Hey Hey it's time to fight,
Everybody
yell blue and white (or any colours).
BLUE AND WHITE!
Hey hey let's do it again
Everybody yell GO FIGHT WIN
Go, Fight, Win!
Go, Fight, Win!

Before I knew it, the cheerleaders were in action shouting 'Hey! Hey! Hey!' at the top of their voices.

Gosh! Where on earth had I landed? I could have been at home curled up in bed with Jojo, instead of this manic party where everyone seemed to be warming up to spending an entire night rocking away. But by now the singing had started and mikes had been dug out. The crowd was at it, with all gusto. Each time one of the groups delayed in giving their song, the cheerleaders would rush in and shout:

> 'Hey! Hey! Hey!
> There is aaaaaaaa delay.
> Better watch out or you'll be out.'

Then the letter 'h' came to the men's side. Since 'h' songs had been sung too many times, I was hopeful that this marked the end of the contest and the cheerleading. The cheerleaders were just rushing in when someone cleared his throat, and in all that confusion, sang the first lines of a song starting with 'h'. A soft, lovely and utterly romantic song from the film *Aashiqui 2* which could turn me mooney-eyed despite the innumerable times I had heard the track. Somehow the crowd was lulled into silence and the singer went full throttle into the song, sonorously belting out, 'Kyunki tum hi ho, tum hi ho, zindagi ab tum hi ho.'

'Wah! Wah! Wah! Full song please,' came the appreciative cries. One of my former classmates poked me in the stomach and hissed, 'That's your fellow singing. How romantic, yaar!'

Oh dear. The voice belonged to Venkat! He was singing so beautifully that the entire crowd was in raptures. I was really amazed to hear him. Someone started to strum a guitar and the entire mood shifted. We moved to softer and lighter songs, and on popular demand, Venkat moved to another uber romantic song which had me tingling. While singing, Venkat had moved his gaze towards my direction. The crowd too had sensed that the song was being sung for me. The mood was charged, and I felt myself being drawn into it.

But then I shook myself. Maybe the atmosphere was such that I was beginning to imagine things. Next week I was to be off to Delhi for further studies and it was time to say goodbye to Bareilly, Venkat and whatever emotions that were possibly obstacles in my larger goal.

So, at some moment, I slipped out and made for home. I left behind a starry night, sounds of dreamy singing and several unanswered questions.

18

D-DAY

Focused as I was on the mother-of-all-exams, I pushed off to Delhi the very next day. Was I running away from the feelings that I had for Venkat? Maybe. But emotions be damned! I was so near to Baba's goal. My recent visit to Bareilly had opened my eyes to the fact that status and standing in society came from having a good government job and being an officer. My parents had suffered enough in life by not being the crème de la crème of society and there were too many ambitions vested in me, which was perhaps an obligation on my part to fulfill. Therefore, no distractions.

I found a room in Mukerjee Nagar and moved in with two other girls while preparing for the imminent interview. Somehow, I had a feeling that I stood a good chance of getting a call for the interview. Although, first-timers qualifying the exam are rare and that too with my kind of focus. One of my roommates would visit the Hanuman Mandir on Thursdays to pray and I started to tag along. So that was how I got introduced to her astrologer; a tacky road-side fellow, but she swore by him. The man looked at my chart, made a few noises and then announced that good news was to come my way in case I was looking for a job. Boy! Was I thrilled!

The chances that things would come together for me seemed bright and the results confirmed my optimism. Yes! I had made it to the interview list. Baba was weeping all over the phone and Bhai was grinning non-stop.

'Just the last stage,' Baba said to me. 'And you are through the exam.'

Interviews were about two months away. I stood a 50:50 chance but recollecting Misraji's account of the process, there stood a better chance for me as a woman candidate. All I needed was to keep my wits and be abreast with the latest developments.

Wits were critical here. Misraji had told me of several candidates who made it through just on that basis. Like the chap who topped the exams a few years ago. His interview was going miserably and one of the board members asked him in sheer exasperation, 'Tell me, why at all you were born?'

Pat came the response, 'Sir, I was not consulted by my parents!'

So, you see, wits, wits and more wits.

So I trotted off to the institute to seek out Misraji and get more dope. The kind of information I got was enough to put me in a quandary. You need to prepare for anything. For one they quiz you on the form you fill; then whatever you say leads to another query. Like the candidate who was asked to name four Indian economists, which he did. But the next question shot at him was whether he knew who Samuelson was, which he didn't. He covered it up instead by saying that he only knew one Samuelson who plays for the West Indian Cricket team! Good enough because he scored well and ended up making it to the top 200. Another candidate entered the boardroom and fell flat on ground. The chairman uttered, 'Mr what a great fall!' The candidate stood up, smiled and responded, 'Sir, it's a pleasure to have fallen in the company of great men like you.'

Misraji recollected the interview of an ex-student from the institute who mentioned that classical singing was his hobby and was asked to sing a song. Then he was asked to sing the same song in different raga. The candidate was able to do that and got really high marks.

I goggled and read up on as many interview experiences as possible but really couldn't think of what and how to prepare. I banked upon a clear head on the fateful day to see me through.

However, no one had forewarned me that my interview would be a family outing. Ma and Baba landed up, and then we had family conferences in which Sweety gave her pearls of wisdom.

'What will Meena wear?' was her first query. 'My friend who got 20th rank last year wore a handloom print draped gracefully and was complimented by the interview board too.'

As my experience in wearing saris was next to nil, she took it upon herself to clothe me in one. I weakly protested that it might fall off, but to no avail.

Next item on the agenda was how haggard I looked these days. 'Look at your face!' everyone said. 'Seems like a convict has just come out of jail!' Obviously I'd look haggard if the entire hopes of the other four at the table rested upon my performance at the interview. Clearly, the burden on me was onerous, being the first of this khandaan to hit big time. But Sweety had a solution for that too. She strictly informed me that I was to accompany her for a facial and skin clean-up the day before the interview. *Noooooooooo…* I protested, but could do so only mentally, as the other four seemed to have ganged up.

I missed Jojo. He'd have been on my side for sure; here,

I had to turn to discussions in which the family passed some sort of resolution that henceforth I'd scrub my face daily till the interview day, apply a fruit pack, freshly cut tomato, a dab of honey, throw in multani mitti and eureka! I have an altogether new addition to Misraji's things-to-do before the IAS interview list. I'd also practise smiling in front of the mirror for my really scant dimples to be visible prominently.

So the D-day, arrived. Ma gave me a onceover; she was teary eyed at my so-called revived and glowing complexion, and my starched and pinned sari and sensible sandals (more power to Sweety as she had fulfilled her role as Bahu admirably). I hadn't slept the entire night. Ma did a round of the puja thaal, shoved a big laddoo in my mouth and handed over the Hanuman Chalisa, brought specifically from Bareilly for this event, to hold during the drive to UPSC. For some reason, Bhai wanted to take a snap of all of us before we left. He ended up taking a selfie, which I was pretty sure captured most of us with grimacing faces, barring Sweety who looked, well, sweet as always.

Bhai by now had acquired a car. Sweety's dad gave it as a wedding present. If you ask me, I disapproved of the damn thing as it was dowry; the two of them would have married regardless of the car. But right now, I was getting into the car, in the front seat so that my sari would not crush, while the parents and Sweety squeezed into the rear.

Time to hit the road!

We reached the UPSC office at around eight o' clock. As that was way before the interview time, Bhai drove down to the bylane near the UPSC office, and the agonizing wait till 9 a.m. started. Baba appeared more nervous than me, while Ma was, as usual, a picture of inscrutable composure though her lips were silently moving as though she was reciting a non-stop prayer. Sweety chose to give her enlightened views on the guys and gals waiting like us. 'Hey, this chaat shop looks interesting! What say, Meena?'

I was really irritated at that solidly trivial comment but I let it be and practised pranayam to calm down. I took deep breaths. Ooooomm…deep breath. And then another Ooom. It frankly didn't work. Distracting thoughts ran through my mind and I was a total bundle of nerves.

At 8:50 a.m. we drove towards the UPSC gate and everyone in the car got into a tizzy as no one knew where to park. While the family figured it out, I sat back, AC on full blast because the starch in the sari had begun to itch.

At nine o'clock the candidates were let in. While dashing towards the gate, I accidentally left my call letter in the car and tripping over my sari, I rushed back to the car. UPSC turned out to be nice, quiet air-conditioned building exuding a sense of timelessness and calm. Once the formalities at the reception were over, the candidates were herded into the waiting hall—a big, circular room with a dome-shaped ceiling. The lighting had a pleasant yellowish hue. We sat around eight wooden low roundtables with six chairs at each table where an elderly looking gentleman checked our documents.

I initiated conversation with fellow candidates. There were two doctors (both second-timers), one engineer and one lawyer who were first-timers like me but better qualified and not merely a History Honours degree holder. Did I stand a chance against this lot with their degrees and experience? But no negative thoughts were to be entertained at this critical time, and suddenly I thought of Venkat. He too must've gone through this drill. Perhaps he sat on the same chair as mine. That, certainly, was a comforting thought. Then the next thought rushed in that he had not even wished me for the interview. Swat went that thought!

Somehow all of that kept my nervousness at bay. I clutched the Hanuman Chalisa tightly in my hand as I stared intently at the slow, rotating ceiling fan. Frankly, if the Government of India looked anything like the UPSC building, then I would be in clover if I qualified. The only odd notes were the UPSC employees who looked tired and weather-beaten with their indeterminate colour attire. If I qualify, I'm going to put in a cheerful dress code for all employees, I thought. We were offered tea and biscuits, which I happily gobbled as I'd given breakfast a go by.

My turn for the interview was second last. One Mr Know-all was the last and this was his fourth interview. He would assess the candidates as they were called one by one: 'Iska to sure-shot hai (he will get through for sure)', he'd say, or shake his head at another candidate. When it was just the two of us left in the room, he declared that I could treat this interview as a test practice for next time! Between the starchy sari, the six biscuits and his non-stop commentary, I was once again a bundle of nerves when my turn came.

Let it suffice to say that the interview went off well. I followed a famous person's policy which we were taught in our public speaking session at school. The guest speaker had told us that he'd practised public speaking by addressing a field full of cauliflowers; thereafter, whenever he needed to address any gathering, the audience would be cauliflowers for him! So it was that the six people on the board were speaking cauliflowers for me. One asked me my name. Another quizzed me a bit about my subject. The toughest was the harsh-looking Madam who asked me where my sari was from. 'Not sure. My sister-in-law bought it from me. Where exactly she bought it from I don't know,' I replied. Then I added helpfully, 'If you want I can find out and let you know.'

The lady clammed up, her mouth a tight line, but the gentlemen sitting on her right very nicely clarified that what the lady board member had meant was which part of the country the sari was from. I was comfortable with that one because Sweety had debated at length on the sari and whether it should be Bengali cotton or a Coimbatore cotton, and so on. More questions were asked on the region from where the sari came, on Bareilly. And yes, yes yes! I sent a mental thanks to Sunita and my ex-gang of Bareillyites as a question was also posed to me on Bollywood film songs based on Bareilly.

Fifteen minutes later I was out, relieved that the first interview of my life was over. I moved out towards my waiting family. They were eager for details but my response was low key. The feeling hit me that an ordeal of several months was over. Moreover, the psychological pressure behind this entire exam had been simmering in my life for long. Finally, I could take a break until the next time, if at all.

19

I CLIMBED THE EVEREST

With little to do and lots of time on hand, I decided to return to Bareilly with my parents. With no friends in Delhi with whom I could consider unwinding, and disconnected from mobile and internet since months, I was really cut off from the world of normal humans. Better to return, be with the parents, enjoy Jojo's company and generally pass time pottering around the house. The sense of vacuum was huge. Maybe, I should give myself a break and start preparing for the next attempt in a short while.

I slept and slept and slept all the way back home, in the train and thereafter at home. Jojo, unaccustomed to this, licked me to wakefulness early next morning. Rolling out of bed, I decided to take him out for a run. The world looked fresh to me without the tension of having to ceaselessly study or think about studying. Despite the summer heat, the smell of the amaltas flowers glorious in their yellow hue, and the red jacaranda flowers, hit my senses. There had been no sanity all these months with the onerous burden of studies. Now the luxury of time was heavenly.

But things in our household are never stable. Baba came

home one afternoon early from work, tension writ large on his face.

'I've been transferred out of Bareilly,' he announced.

'Why on earth?' Ma and I asked. 'Your retirement is barely a few years away.'

Baba had fallen out with some senior at work. This was a punishment transfer. There was no solution except to push hard and make serious effort to have the order reversed. Suddenly, I could sense Baba's aging. The years of worrying and care had taken their toll on his health; this movement was really out of the question. We debated the options. The easiest was that he resigns. He had built a small-ish house on the outskirts of Bareilly and that was a comfort. But what played on his mind was my situation. Bhai had somehow climbed up the legal hierarchy and his father-in-law had had him fixed with a Supreme Court firm. But I was unmarried, and so far, 'unsettled', and was a responsibility for which he as yet had to cater for financially.

Therefore, ideally, some intervention was required.

'Venkat,' said Ma. 'I'm sure he can help. He must be having some contacts at the Health Department. I think that we call him.'

I sort of froze at that. It's a different thing knowing a person casually, but to seek a favour of him was something I couldn't swallow. Then, there was also that last unfinished meeting between us. I thought to myself that we wait a bit before deciding to give him a call.

It was a restless night with none of us sleeping much. Baba was to join in a month's time, so decisions would be made in due course. Also, my results were expected within that period and some decisions pended on that outcome.

So, it was to be a period of uncertainty. Frankly, too much seemed to rest on me. Though I had unquestioningly accepted this responsibility or, calling it expectation, all these years, a wee bit of frustration had started to creep in. Why does the entire family have to focus on some sort of growth spurt and status uplift if I qualify for the IAS? At the end of the day, it would only be a talking point that our daughter/niece/sister is in the IAS. What sort of elevation would that effectively translate into?

I wished to have someone to talk to. The house was totally in a pressure cooker situation. Being home meant being surrounded by gloom. Being out meant hanging on your own. So I turned to the internet for solace and for company. I tried connecting with old college buddies and found two or three groups which I could join. Of course, some of the sickos like Sudhir were in the groups, but there was a limit to which I could be picky. In fact, I was surprised to receive a good luck message from Raghu. I guess with passage of time relationships ease out. I tried unsuccessfully to locate Venkat on Facebook. Obviously, he had views on social networking too! I did seriously want to touch base with him again now that I was free. One couldn't overlook that he had really played a huge role in giving me advice for these exams. Of course, instead of sending him a message, I could have just as well gone across to his office, a stone's throw away. But unsure of his reaction, I abandoned that idea.

I guess I just didn't do much but hang around. Meanwhile, a friend of Baba's offered him a job at his recently opened hospital at Bareilly. Baba was now preparing to resign from his job, and Ma was busy with packing and moving on.

My result came on 6 June. I was as usual on the internet

and found that the UPSC site had become heavy and was repeatedly hanging. It was clear that the results had come! I waited a while wanting to postpone the inevitable. A race of thoughts went thorough me: what if I didn't qualify? How will I cope with failure? Did I at all stand a chance?

All this while I continued to hit away at the keyboard and got into a mass of windows. Extricating myself, several moments later, I found that the UPSC site flashed open. I fed my roll number: 036363. The computer flashed rank 12. Blinking, I thought it must be an error. So I re-checked. Again the rank flashed was 12. Not possible, I thought, and checked again. Meanwhile, my mobile went ping, another ping and then ping, ping, ping. Then the phone went into a crescendo of ringtones. I sat on my chair paralyzed.

'Jojo,' I said. 'I think I've made it!' In my excitement I accidentally pressed hard at Jojo lying at my feet, which had him in whimpers. I asked him, 'Okay. If you wag your tail, Jojo, then I'll consider it a good omen.'

No response.

So, I opened the door to my room, then shut it, then opened it again, tried the UPSC site again and got the same result. Next, I shut down the PC, restarted it and checked once more. Same result. I was anxious as hell. This was something I couldn't get wrong. How to re-check? I peered at my mobile and saw several missed calls and then one message flashed from Misraji. It just said, 'Congratulations! Congratulations! Congratulations!' Yes, the Everest of exams, the IAS, had been successfully climbed by me. It was time to face the world with the glad tidings.

I took a printout of the result and walked slowly towards the kitchen where Ma had been preparing dinner. 'Ma,' I said simply, handing over the printout to her. Sometimes words are unnecessary.

As she read the result tears welled up; never seen her so emotional. She hugged me tight and then just wept. The phone now couldn't be ignored. Bhai, Sweety, Sweety's parents, Misraji. Endless calls were waiting to be answered. Baba was yet to be informed. He was probably on his way home, which meant that I shouldn't call on his mobile as yet. A little later the car came in. I went out and wordlessly handed him the result. It was his dream that I had realized, and it was important for me that he savours it fully. I thought that Baba was the happiest man on earth that day. He read the result, patted me on my back, read it again, wiped his eyes; perhaps we were finally a content family.

It was party time thereafter. The world and its amma made way to our house: endless mithai, cups of tea, ceaseless chatter. By late night I was so tired that I hit the sack immediately.

Next morning was different when I woke up. Was it a dream, I thought, and took out the paper with my result. No, it was true and I was now confirmed as an IAS officer. Yes! Yes! Yes! The Bareilly newspaper blazoned the headlines that I had made it big. Soon, the reporters were seeking my interview.

'Wear something decent,' trilled Sweety from Delhi at me.

So I fished out a respectable salwar kameez, put on light make-up and gave the very first interview of my life in the presence of my parents and Jojo. Well, the questions were pretty obvious and I had decided to give pretty much the same replies as earlier successful candidates. (Google baba zindabad!) But then I don't know what got into me all of a sudden when the journalist asked, 'So Meena, who was your real inspiration, both in life as well as for this exam?'

'Mahatma Gandhi was an inspiration since childhood,' was my response, 'and more recently, I was really inspired by someone who is going to be my colleague in the IAS, an officer senior to me. You know he is posted in Bareilly and really mentored me through the process.'

Baba jerked up, his glasses fell on his nose. Ma gave a sigh, this girl will never change was her visible expression. Too late to retract, I clammed up.

20

MADAM BUSYBODY SPOILS THE FUN

And the morning after, when I woke up, there was an SMS from the man I had spoken about to the local press yesterday. 'Thanks,' it read, 'and heartiest congratulations! You deserve it.' Venkat had reappeared in my life and it made me happy, happy enough to respond, 'Let's meet and celebrate!'

'Yes,' came the prompt response, followed by, '6:30 at the Bareilly Club?'

So we met at the club. He was a wee bit stiff as he entered the lounge area, our last meeting clouding his mind, but soon we got chatting as though there had been no odd moments between us. He wanted the details of the interview and went over them minutely while I relished his interest in my life. Coffee led to dinner and then looking at his watch he asked, 'How will you go home?'

'I don't know...I came by auto, will look for one to return...'

But by then his lal-batti car was in the drive and we both got in. Suddenly, things stiffened up again, and both of us spoke at the same time, 'I...I...' he said, while I uttered, 'Youuuu ...' I don't know what he must've been thinking because the next minute he invited me to come along with him on a trip to Nainital. He had a meeting to attend and would drive there, stay a night and return the next evening. Would I be keen? 'Most certainly', was my enthusiastic response. And after having responded, the terrible load of having to inform my parents that I was going on an overnight trip with Venkat, albeit an innocent one, hit me. How on earth would I work that out?

I reached home to find more people flooding our drawing room. By now, even Ma's enthusiasm for dishing out endless cups of tea and snacks was flagging. We slept late at night, and I missed Baba the next morning before he left for work. But I woke up feeling fresh, as though the entire world looked new. Was it the relief that there was no more studying to do or was it my imminent trip with Venkat?

Ma and I were having our mid-morning tea, and as I awaited an opportunity to tell her about the trip, yet another nosy-parker well-wisher walked in full of felicitations and looking as if she'd come with the intent of settling down for a longish chat. Madam Busybody seemed to be well-informed on what happens to an IAS officer after qualifying the exam.

'Ranks hardly matter,' she said. 'What matters is your cadre, the state you are posted. After all, you have to spend a lifetime in the allotted state, don't you? '

'Ab IAS trainees ko cadres jaldi allot ho jate hain (IAS trainees get cadres soon), within few months of joining the service,' she continued, 'machine se. You can get any cadre and it's all luck. Be prepared for anything from Nagaland to Kerala. Despite your rank, you can't be sure where you'll land.'

Ma started to look worried. This was something she had never reckoned for all this while. What if I didn't get my home state despite my rank?

But relief was in sight as our visitor doled out more gyan on the subject.

'But there is always a solution for this situation. Agar pasand ka cadre nahin milta hai to phir CBM ek tarika hai (If you don't get your home state then CBM is a way out).'

CBM? Neither of us knew what that meant. I asked innocently, 'What is CBM, Aunty?'

'Arre, imtihaan pass kar gayi lekin CBM ke baare mein nahin suna? Couples from All India Services are allowed to change their cadre to that of their spouse or any third cadre, if they both agree. That is why a lot of CBMs (Cadre Based Marriages) happen in the academy. All one has to do is to find a right match...in the right state...'

Oh no was my instinctive response. This was likely to open up a floodgate of tension and planning in my family. I could already sense that Ma was desperate for more details. And Aunty was more than willing to provide them.

'Well it can be a dream come true, a nightmare, or somewhere in between the two for many. There is not much of a choice in the selection of cadre and only a few are lucky enough to get their own states as their cadre. Then a young IAS is posted in little known districts. The job involves heavy workload, frequent tours to rural hinterland and immense pressures. There is huge power and prestige, but it can be a lonely journey. Officers are provided large kothis, government vehicles (with a beacon), armed security, servants, etc. They are vested with a good amount of power and authority, which brings a lot of social recognition. But one gets used to this and the charm lasts for a year or two. Then you and your family start worrying. After all, every girl is born to get married, produce children and have companionship.'

She had by now pretty much figured out that in Ma there was a captive audience. We could now connect the dots as to how a colleague of Baba had become hyper-tense after his daughter was allotted a far away cadre, and who rued the day that his child even took the exam. To make matters worse, the girl was still unwed.

'It's true that for a boy his value in the marriage market shoots up overnight,' Aunty continued. 'Ab you can say that there is more to life than getting married to the highest bidder. But bina dahej ke shaadi kaun karta hai? (Who marries without dowry)? However, the marriage prospects for a lady officer are diametrically opposite. While the males are busy selecting the "right" girl out of hundreds, the lady officer has to choose from a very limited pool of officers. Arre bhai, you can't marry an officer to a clerk can you? Thankfully, there is a simple way out. The government policy is to allot the same cadre to couples, which results in a lot of CBMs.'

Aunty had succeeded in bursting Ma's bubble. All that happiness went out from her 'puff', as I looked on in sheer horror. I wished, just wished that Aunty had come in another day and let Ma enjoy my results a bit more.

After she had left I told Ma not to worry. But I can make out her mood from the way she moves the pots and pans in the kitchen—it was back to silent despondency. Baba came in a bit later and she narrated the entire morning's conversation to him. From my room I could hear them talk in low tones, with overtones of tension. This too shall pass, I thought and emerged only at lunchtime. From my point of view, what was the point of worrying about something that one can't control. And then the cadre allotment was too far away to disturb my peace of mind as yet. Tab ki tab dekhi jayegi (I'll face things when they happen). So, at lunch I thought of changing the topic and broke the news of Venkat's invitation to accompany him on an inspection.

Pin-drop silence greeted me. Maybe they were upset? Annoyed? Displeased? I saw Baba open and shut his mouth like a goldfish. Flashes of an emotion that I couldn't fathom played across his face. I also saw a curiously shuttered look come over him but the words he articulated were, 'Good, that's not a bad idea. You'll get a firsthand experience of the job that you are getting into.'

So I wrote an SMS to Venkat that our trip was on and returned to surfing with Jojo at my feet.

21

THROWING CAUTION TO THE WINDS

To put it in black and white, it was a dream trip. And yes, short of making love, we did all the loving that we could. After all, what else does one expect to happen when one is single, full of hormones and in a balmy environment like Nainital?

Early in the trip I figured out that Venkat was going to finally come out with something about us. He was looking cool and thoroughly relaxed in an olive green T-shirt and jeans. Somewhere during the journey, I dozed off and woke up to find my head resting on his shoulder. I let it be there. He knew I was awake and lifted a hand to gently remove a strand of hair from my face. His fingers lightly brushed at my breasts. I held my breath, but it was the driver in the car who stymied any further action between us. I was left with a curling feeling in my stomach, a gush of longing that he should let his hand be and...

We took a break after some time to freshen up and have breakfast. Ma had packed some food for us so we thought of moving into the shaded space behind the PWD house to eat. Eating though was far from my mind. Venkat's too. He called out for me 'Hey! Come and see this room.' As I entered, he grabbed me from behind the door and pulled me into his arms. After that we kissed really long and hard until someone politely knocked at the door to inform us that the tea was ready.

At Nainital, we were put up at the Circuit House in adjacent rooms, and though Nainital is a beautiful place, I frankly didn't care to see much of it. All we did was hold hands and walk miles. The weather was misty and the clouds were drifting. Light drizzle and holding hands made us a couple indeed! At night, Venkat found his way to my room and snuggled into bed with me. We kissed and caressed. I moaned repeatedly while Venkat shushed me, warning me that the sounds would carry in the silence of the night. But there was no stopping. I was high, and having a job with a man to love was a double bonus. It seemed as if the gods above had started to take note that there was this creature down below that'd really needed a boost in the goodies department!

But Venkat is an honourable man. Against my wishes, he pushed me away, gently admonishing that things could wait until later. Later when, I cried? Whenever, but not that night. So I was a bit peeved that he made off into his room leaving me all aroused and abandoned.

There was no time for sulking with him though and the next morning we made off to the nearby hills—this time Venkat was behind the wheels, giving the driver a break. We'd take shelter when it rained in small roadside teashops and chat to our heart's content. I found out a bit about his family. I learnt how he had been brought up as a single child to diplomat parents that led him to have a good international exposure; about his grandparents who lived in Coonoor and with whom he stayed to study for the IIT and later the Civil Services until he finally moved to Delhi. We exchanged little bits about each other but more him than me. In my case he was already on familiar territory and had most of the information. Like a person in love, I was besotted by the little details about him: where he studied, what he liked to eat, what he read, the music he liked, etc. It was bliss.

The return back to Bareilly was heart wrenching. We wouldn't be so free to meet and be with each other in that town but going back was inevitable. It was only later, much much later, that I figured out how Venkat had thrown caution to the winds by taking a trip like this with me. To romance in a sarkari workplace is like making a public announcement of a relationship to the junta at large and giving rise to rumours and malicious chit chat. There is little room for private space in a sarkari environment. But more of that later.

I returned home looking very much a woman in love. Something had changed and that was visible to my parents, I think. But lost in my thoughts, I made off with Jojo and crashed out.

22

ROYALLY STUMPED

*N*ext morning there was a panic call from Bhai. Sweety had had a fall and was hospitalized with a hip fracture. So we rushed off to Delhi. As it appeared that the hospitalization would be of a long duration, I opted for hospital duty while Ma returned home with Baba. So Venkat and I had to make do with phone calls and SMSes. In any case, I'd started to figure out that he was not only honourable, but also extremely reticent. While I could rattle on and on about the hospital and Sweety and her pain and even the dosage of the medicine she was taking, little information would be forthcoming from the other end. An easy query like 'how was your day?' would be met with a short response: 'okay'. And that would be that.

I really started to wonder about him. Now that I was heady with success and beginning a new chapter in my life, his over cautious and staid approach was a solid bugging thing for me, and I told him so. To which he simply laughed and said, 'You've to mature a lot.' Gosh this man is irritating! But still we would coo over the phone and I'd end up invariably telling him how much I missed him.

Three weeks into this Sweety was discharged and almost

simultaneously a letter came for me from the government carrying general instructions about joining the Mussoorie academy. Misraji wickedly had informed that the communication would carry instructions to the effect like whether or not trainees can use mobile phones, or whether a lady officer trainee (OT) compulsorily needs to wear a sari 'in sobre colours'. What if an OT is found drinking whiskey? He was, as usual, bang on. Some babu had drafted these instructions for future OTs:

1. Officer trainees are strictly prohibited from using mobile phones in the academic area. There are written instructions that mobile phones found with OTs in the academic area would be confiscated, and the officer fined. Trainees are however allowed to use mobile phones in their hostel rooms.

2. An officer trainee found in possession of alcohol or found to be in an inebriated condition would not be allowed to continue the course with immediate effect. This will also invite disciplinary action against the would-be-officer.

3. The three-month-long Foundation Course is a 'no leave' course. That means no leave is granted during this period. Before joining the academy, OTs are advised to settle matters requiring their personal presence.

4. First special salary advance is admissible after completion of one month of training. That means, everyone needs to bring sufficient money for one month's expenses.

5. On formal occasions, gentlemen OTs need to wear a black or white buttoned-up suit or black sherwani with white churidar pyjamas and formal black shoes (oxfords or brogues only) with black socks. The first such occasion is the inauguration of the Foundation Course itself. Gentlemen OTs are also required to wear formal lounge suits (preferably of darker colours) with neckties on certain prescribed occasions.

6. So far as lady OTs are concerned, the dress code is sari (but mind it 'in sober colours') with formal shoes or sandals.

7. Even in classrooms, one can't just walk in wearing a T-shirt. Gentlemen OTs are required to wear full sleeve shirts and trousers with neckties (summer) and jackets and trousers with neckties (winter) with formal shoes.

8. And for lady OTs, the classroom dress code is saris/salwar kameezes/churidar kurtas/western business suits with formal shoes or sandals.

Get a life man! These instructions belonged to some way out era. How does one survive without a mobile? But, after all, while studying for the exams one didn't even switch on one's mobile, so I guess that was adequate practice. The sari bit was also frightening. I think I've worn a sari precisely thrice in my lifetime. In fact, in Bareilly, I had availed the services of a beauty parlour which charged ₹250 for tying a sari, which I had to wear for a friend's wedding. I guess I'd have to invest in some formal Indian wear or practise wearing a sari and also buy some woolies. And also take a loan from Baba for the initial month.

Venkat called as I was making my list. He helpfully clarified that I ignore the bits in the letter which sounded as if we were entering a convent school.

'When do you join?' he asked.

'1st of September.'

'Will you come to Bareilly before that?'

'Of course,' I retorted immediately.

I had to go back as we had to move house and Ma could do with some help.

'Actually,' he continued, and mind you, I could sense that his tone had changed, 'I wanted us to go to Coonoor before you joined the academy.'

'Coonoor? Why there?'

Not realizing that there was something more to his invitation than my dumb brain could figure out, I continued.

'Look, Venkat, I have a billion things to do before I leave and my parents are shifting and these will be my last few moments with them before I join work.'

And I went on and on and on.

A longish silence later, Venkat simply said, 'Somehow, I'd thought we could formalize things and take them forward between us before you joined the academy. And for that it would've been good if you met my family first.'

I was stumped, royally stumped. Honestly, our relationship had hardly reached any such stage that we went around announcing it, let alone formalizing things and then, all we had done was to neck a bit which was, in a typical Venkat-ish manner, taken to the next level.

So, there was little choice but to stall things which I think I did ham-handedly; he abruptly disconnected the phone with a terse 'bye' and that was the end of that.

23

THAT ROMEO–JULIET TYPE THING

So guiltily, the first thing I did on reaching Bareilly was
to make way to Venkat's office. It looked like a slow, old-
fashioned and very unhappy place—a contrast to the UPSC
building in Delhi. I crossed the barriers and security guards
who appeared totally unsure about whether to welcome me in
or keep me out. However, only when I got past all that stuff
could I enter the building.

Someone led me to Venkat's room. There were people with
him, so I sat in a corner sofa chair disapprovingly surveying the
damp, infested walls, the picture of the President, the lop-sided
air conditioner and the wilting flowers in a brass flower pot. The
chairs were dusty and the covers a suspicious brown. Venkat's
table was massive, megalomaniacal in proportions and covered
in some sort of a green cloth. There were tonnes of paper on
it. Two plastic trays were labelled 'IN' and 'OUT'. What really
added to the depressive atmosphere were the cupboards that
lined the room, dense wooden cupboards full of papers and
files and books. Given that it was my first visit to the place,
my immediate reaction was of sheer horror: there and then I
wanted to run away. Oblivious to my presence, the 2–3 people

sitting across his table continued chatting and laughing while Venkat himself seemed to be attending numerous phone calls.

A while later everyone left but for a girl who Venkat introduced to me.

'Leela, my batchmate. Leela, meet Meena, she has qualified the IAS this year and is about to join the academy.'

'Congratulations!' effused the lady. 'And welcome to this mad bad world of IAS officers.'

That's when I got put off by her and that's also when I got around to looking at her properly. Clad in a chiffon sari, a semi-transparent one, Leela had bright eyes, pouting red lips, a voluptuous figure and painted nails. I felt like sitting on my hands to hide the unpolished look that I normally sport. As she made no signs of leaving the room I moved to the table to join them. The conversation turned to their days at the academy which pretty much alienated me from their world of shared experiences.

'Remember CD? Such a creep! I heard later that he beat his wife,' Leela said.

Hello? What on earth is a CD? Should I ask, butt in perhaps? I eventually did and meekly asked, 'CD? Are the classes held through electronic mode?'

Leela convulsed into laughter as though it was the best joke that she had heard in years.

'Ha! You have a hope in hell. Nothing even remotely electronic about that place. Only thing electronic...'

Venkat gently intervened to clarify that the faculty was mainly of serving IAS officers with a decade or so of service and that CD, far from being an electronic item, stood for course director, who would pretty much rule our lives for the duration of the time we'd spend in training.

'Yaar, tell the truth. The faculty consists of all sorts of IAS officers who cool it out in the academy. It's a closed type of environment there with a different set of problems. We had some really complex personalities there, you know those types who really couldn't do much in the service and all that...,' said Leela.

'Not really, not true actually,' said Venkat.

'Come on, yaar! All that the faculty did was snoop on us instead of giving gyan on public service delivery. Remember Misra and his wife Misrain?'

And Leela burst into more derisive laughter. Venkat made yet another futile interjection that he didn't notice any snooping, etc., and that in any organization there will be all sorts of personalities to tackle but to little effect. Obviously, Leela was not only opinionated but extremely sure that her world vision was the best. I wondered briefly how she herself was as an officer.

So I thought it was time to leave and got up. Obviously, the two of them were on a wavelength which didn't correspond with mine.

Venkat came home that evening, No time for private conversation, but he mentioned that he was off to Coonoor for a holiday and that probably he wouldn't be posted back in Bareilly when he returned. Now, did I sense a distance when he said that? I walked him to the gate where his car was parked and on impulse I whispered, 'Will you take me for a ride?'

And before we both knew, we had reached an isolated road and were all over each other. 'God!' I heard him moan, 'how much I've missed you. Come with me to Coonoor, please. Meet my people. I'll speak with your parents that we wish to get married.'

Marriage? The thought had not even crossed my mind. What on earth made him think that I was looking out for getting married to him? Honestly, I didn't know how to react. There, the exciting prospect of joining the academy was looming large and here, someone was asking me to get married. I sort of froze up on Venkat and he was sharp enough to sense my mood. We moved apart and he dropped me home in silence. Not a word was exchanged between us.

Later that night I pondered over my situation. Look, I know I am not stable in the emotions department and tend to zigzag from here to there. But what I figured out at the end of the day was that I am a combo of being glamour-stricken and commitment-shy. Venkat is apparently not at all glamorous and he wants commitment which I am not prepared to give right now. That Romeo–Juliet type thing was not in me that I go around moping for him. Theek hai, if he is around, good, if not, then I'll miss him for sure but not wilt away forever.

24

KEEN TYPE PROBATIONER OR MAST INVISIBLE TYPE PROBATIONER?

I had, long ago, stuck pics of Lal Bahadur Shastri National Academy of Administration (LBSNAA) on the walls of my room. They had occupied pride of place on my walls. I would constantly look at them for inspiration. Now, it was almost time to pack my bags for LBSNAA and live the reality. I felt very proud that I was entering a life and a service full of challenges and responsibilities. It was also time to help Ma and Baba move into our new house.

A tearful goodbye later, I made way for Dehradun alone (resisting Baba's insistence to accompany me). It was raining heavily, which made for a gloomy atmosphere. Though the drive up the hills was scenic, the entry into Mussoorie and later into the academy wasn't too thrilling. Chaotic traffic at the entry road meant that it took forty minutes to cover just about half a km to reach the academy. The gate of LBSNAA, which I had been using as a screen saver on my laptop, was dimly visible in the rain and I was seriously disappointed that it was like any other gate, with a small board announcing that this indeed was the academy. The reality didn't live up to my expectations, and the rain made it difficult to click a pic. I was upset.

I met my roommate who, to put it mildly, was a total put-off. More rain followed; by now, my enthusiasm was seriously dampened. The room itself was no great shakes. Listlessly I strolled out of my room after depositing my luggage and I could spot other probationers entering the the place with their baggage, etc. As I knew no one else who had qualified the exam that year, I reckoned there was no point in assessing anyone then. Enough time for that later.

To change my mood, I changed clothes, got into a newly tailored outfit and decided to eat. The climb to the mess was steep; I was anticipating mint-fresh probationers in bandhgalas and starched saris eating delicately and self-consciously with forks and spoons. Excuse me? Can you kindly pass me the salt, please? Thank you. Ultimate shishtachar. But instead,the mess had people from varied parts of the country, some really old-looking, some looked as though uttering even one word of English minus the regional accent would be a huge triumph! Pretty much an extension of the training institute crowd. Mentally I could imagine Venkat shaking his head at me and reprimanding, what else did you expect? What image had you built up in your mind that you are feeling disappointed? However, given my mood and the general bleakness of the weather I fell into immediate deep dejection there and then.

The rain, my first introduction to my likely companions, the sense of friendlessness overwhelmed me and I put my head in my pillow and wept late into the night. Yes, I was definitely homesick.

As per the schedule given to us, we were to wake up

between a 4:45 and 5:30 next morning which my roommate and I did to the sounds of cell phone alarms. Somewhere in the Happy Valley grounds where the academy is located, a shrill whistle sounded repeatedly as room boys rang the doorbells with the call, 'Chai, Sir/Chai, Ma'am.' One by one, groggy officer trainees made their way down the slopes and to the polo grounds. We made an effort in exchanging sleepy greetings.

It became the morning routine subsequently. P.T. with exhortations from the instructors, while the dawn broke across the sky. In fact, on a clear day we could see snow peaks in the distance. The horse riding, a truly colonial legacy, ensured that we returned with aches and pains to our rooms. One fall from the horse and the junta around would snigger and comment, 'See, an ass fallen off the horse!' Upon the cry of 'visarjan'!' we would disperse.

At the very start of the programme, at the academy, we were told the long story of who we were and what we stood for (blah…blah…). Honestly, it didn't make much sense, but I did realize that each one of us stepping out of the academy after our training would have onerous responsibilities on our shoulders. More depression. I'd never ever been alone in this manner and the thought of taking decisions without consulting either Baba or Bhai was frightening. What if I made wrong judgments, totally incorrect choices?

The officer sitting next to me meanwhile scribbled a note which read simply, 'Are you a KTP or an ITP?'

'Dunno. What does that mean?' I scribbled back.

'Keen type probationer or mast invisible type probationer?' came back the note.

Curiously, I took a closer look at my neighbour. Seemed like a smart girl (by the way, all the girls sat together, separate from the men/boys like in a zenana/mardana and the Bareilly parties), and she had a cute-ish smile and sparkling eyes. A hope arose that maybe I would have company in her. I hated my roommate who had long, oiled hair, and the smell of hair oil with strands of hair strewn all over my room was only adding to my miserable state of mind. It didn't help that when I grouched about this to Baba who laughingly countered that were I not used to Jojo's hair all over my room?

It was apparent shortly that the course is no stroll in the park. It demanded 14 to 16 hours of activity a day, which added up to roughly eighty hours a week in academic and other engagements like seminars and discussions. On a typical day, classroom sessions commenced at 9 a.m. There were six academic sessions of fifty-five minutes each. Evenings were usually slotted for sports and cultural programmes before dinner was served at 8 p.m.

Man, are we kids or what?! After slogging it to qualify for the wretched exam, another round of studies appeared. The gods were really unfair.

Shortly it was also apparent that were several types of OTs. There were those whose life mission was to invent excuses for missing PT. Then those who slept peacefully throughout the day in the classes and partied hard most of the night. Then the ones who researched extensively on cadre allotments and future prospects (those were the really spooky types).There were also some serious types, probably the KTPs.

What set the guys and the gals apart was their approach to marriage. True or not, my new found friend defined it for me: First, taking dowry is a foregone conclusion for the guys. Entering into a marriage alliance with a family of a big businessman would ensure money as a sure-shot in one's otherwise resource-parched life. (Yes! There was no way that an officer could cope with the demands of a consumerist India with his salary.) A few guys carried girlfriends from their earlier lives.

For the girls, the deal was reverse.

It is desirable to seek an appropriate spouse in the academy itself, else the chances of leading a single life were solidly bright. Girls were often led up the garden path, sometimes to be abandoned at the altar of dowry or parental disapproval. And the only way one's stock zoomed was at the stage of cadre allotment: get a good cadre and yes! The chances of a CBM would become a distinct possibility.

Amongst the girls, the talk about marriage would be at a feverish pitch. Some had already been through the arranged marriage drill. The experiences narrated ranged from the funny to the bizarre. Like the girl who, in the confines of her room, was told by her prospective groom to reject him as she could do much better. Another batchmate's mother received a brusque phone call from a prospective groom's aunt that they had run a background check on her and had discovered the giveaway evidence of her non-Brahmin eating habits via her Facebook photos: she was merrily waving a chicken leg in the air!

Normally I take time to figure out the lay of the land, but here it was clear that there existed huge mismatch between what I thought I was getting into and the reality. My friend, sensing my reluctance to get into the lets-hook-up-with-a-guy scene asked whether I was in a relationship. I chose to keep quiet and instead silently watched her moves and gave her an ear to share her experiences.

Nothing, nothing at all could perk me up. Yes, I eventually got friendly with a few people and we built some sort of a gang. We'd have late night parties with smuggled booze. We'd sneer at the KTPs who'd put up plays and skits showcasing their dancing or singing in a burst of talent display. But underlying it all was a deep gulf. Despite the mandatory village trip and the lovely ambience, I never got around to getting a sense that yes; I was finally in something that would unleash me into a new world.

A little later, the politics also began. The subtle bitching among the OTs, the potshots taken by the female OTs on a budding romance, the way someone would suddenly stop talking when you entered the CD's room, making you feel that you perhaps were the topic of discussion. It need not have been so. After all, we spent only a few months there, but I guess we are all mere humans at the end of the day.

I wondered how Venkat fared while training here. Maybe his advantage was that he was really comfortable in his own space and skin, unlike me. But still...

25

WHICH WORLD DO THESE GUYS
BELONG TO AFTER ALL?

*W*e were split into different groups for Bharat Darshan. I was separated from my gang and ended up with a bunch with whom communication was really tough. The announcement of the cadres was done just as we left. I was comforted when I was allotted Uttarakhand. That meant contiguity with home. A blessing, truly a blessing. The Cassandras with me, however, were gloomy in their forecast that I would face frightening prospects as some of the regions in the state were remote and really lonely, in addition to being rough in the winters and rainy seasons. I was okay as this was an immensely better alternative to a state far away from home. A devil in me was thrilled that my roommate was allotted Punjab; far, far away from her home state. Everyone was in a tizzy at the allotments, some even ruing the entire process of the exam which would eventually confine them to an unfamiliar territory for most of their professional lives. CD tried to counsel that eventually one learns to adjust to the new environment and actually enjoy it but for the now, whatever he said were mere words.

But the gods had been kind with me this year. Without aligning myself much to the general atmosphere of gloom, I headed for Bareilly. I was dreading visiting our new house.

Baba as usual had a gripe about my cadre allotment. Extremely upset.

'Arre, home state Uttar Pradesh nahin mila,' he grumbled. 'With your rank you should have been allotted your home state.'

I tried getting him to figure out things in a positive light with no success. Frankly, it was too frustrating. I wanted to ask him for what on earth did I take this wretched exam. He had given me a vision of imminent grandeur and luxury and sheer power once I became an IAS officer. But, hello, there was nothing of this sort in sight. Most of the time I was counting the pennies as the guys at the academy had warned us of the miserable pay packages we'd be getting. Therefore, if there was little money in the service, and the future was living in small towns, then what dreams had Baba peddled to me?

I chose to keep quiet like any dutiful daughter. Questioning Baba had never been my scene. We, as a family, had just rolled along as per his whims and fancies, whatever be the outcome. So perhaps he knew a bit more about life than at least I did.

Of course, he knew about life. Next thing I knew, he launched into the subject of cadre based marriages. Breakfast, lunch and dinner the questioning would start about how many couples are getting married in my batch, how many girls have got engaged, how many boys have been allotted Uttar Pradesh, and of whom, how many are unmarried and unhitched, etc. It was so obvious that Baba was desperately shoving me into the direction of a CBM.

Come on, Baba! My mind rebelled. Give me a break! But he was relentless. Ma was quiet as usual but not noiseless, banging away at the dishes, signalling her tension. Frankly, I couldn't figure out what the fuss was all about, it wasn't as though I'd been packed off to the moon. Between Bareilly and Uttarakhand stood a mere half an hour drive. Why was it that they were never ever happy? And also, couldn't they understand that the last year or two had been very stressful for me: so much had come my way, and so much I had to struggle for? Man! One simply needed to sit back and enjoy and not crib and plan ceaselessly…

So with all of this, inevitably, the conversation moved towards Venkat.

'How's Venkat?' asked Baba. 'Are you in touch with him?'

'He's fine. Busy with work. We've exchanged a few messages on and off.'

'No, I think you should make the effort to be closer.'

'Why? I am close enough. As close as the relationship warrants.'

'What happened on that trip the two of you took? The one to Nainital,' was Baba's pointed comeback.

'Baba!' I said. 'Nothing happened. Venkat was on an official tour and I went along to get a free ride to Nainital with him,' I also defiantly retorted, possibly for the first time in my life. 'What exactly do you want to ask of me?'

'Nooo…nothing really.'

And Baba backed off.

At another meal, he again raised the topic of people going around in our batch. This time it was Ma who took up the topic. 'Are you particularly close to anyone in the academy or in your batch? I mean, your father and I want to know if you have developed a fondness for someone. Otherwise we can start looking around for a match.'

'Ma! What's wrong with you? How can I think of marriage? I've barely got in to the job and really can't think of taking another huge decision like marriage?'

'But Meena, you know that that this job is such that if you don't marry now, the chances of finding someone will become difficult later. What's wrong in our thinking in this way for you? Parents only want the best for their children. After all, when you are posted in faraway places and all alone, don't you think your father and I would worry for you? Either of us can't be expected to come and stay with you, we have our own life...'

Okay, I thought. Now I'm under pressure again. Like hell I want to even think of marriage. First that Venkat and his pushing ways, and now my parents. Which world do these guys belong to after all? Who gets married only for the convenience of the family or a cadre choice? I'm just about twenty-five years old and there's still a life awaiting me out there.

On that sour note, I returned for my training, leaving several things unsaid and unsorted between my parents and me.

26

BING!

The thought of district training made me really edgy. I'd be alone in an unknown territory, probably not an uber urban area, and handling situations which were totally new. I was trying to look at the positives. Unlike for most of my batchmates, not much travelling was involved. I merely had to reach Dehradun, down from Mussoorie and then to Rishikesh, fifty-four kilometres away, for the training. Rattling away on the road, fully apprehensive of what lay ahead, I was happy when the phone went bing! Not so happily, I noted that it was a message from Venkat, who had re-surfaced in my life.

'Hi!' Read the message, 'all the best for your training. It will be a great exposure. Do well.'

What is he, my father or some sort of a guru giving me blessings?

Irritated, I replied shortly, 'Thanks. Trust all is well with you.'

'Things are good. I am currently posted at Saharanpur. I wanted to talk to you since long and apologize for having pushed you. It should have struck me that too many things were happening in your life at the time.'

Well how does one reply to guy who is overflowing with the niceties of life; he doesn't drink liquor, doesn't partake coffee or tea, doesn't smoke and even resists from having pre-marital sex. Now he apologizes for my bad behaviour. Gosh! Even Jojo shows more attitude than this guy. Nevertheless, my brief SMS to him was 'It's okay. Let me report for duty and then I'll touch base with you.'

But Venkat persisted, 'Hey! I am only 100-odd kilometres away from your training headquarters. We can easily catch up.'

'Sure.'

In any event, by then I had reached Rishikesh and made way to what was to be my abode for some time. A dingy government building set in a large compound with overgrown plants, a dysfunctional fountain and huge trees which blocked the sun. Not too far away I could hear temple bells, which was some solace as it broke the stillness of the house. The less said about my room the better. It was dark and grayish, the walls painted in an undeterminable colour. An air-conditioner clanged from a window, which had never been cleaned. The small ante-room leading to my bedroom housed a well-used sofa, precariously hanging onto one side. The bedroom was okay and had a TV, a huge relief. What took the cake was the bathroom which was large, spacious and tiled, but dirt caked the tiles as also the wash basin and the loo. Mystifyingly, there was a mug on the floor chained to the tap as if to prevent the occupant of the room from running away with it. A kitchenette completed the set of rooms. There was only one sense the entire suite gave: it hadn't been cleaned in years and that if I spent a minute more in it, I'd suppurate.

I rang the dirty bell lying on the glass-covered table (why on earth was everything brown, including the glass?) The portly attendant who entered my room didn't look encouraging.

'Yeh kamra kab saaf hua tha (When was this room cleaned)?' I asked.

'This morning.'

'But it is filthy and the mattress stinks.'

Silence was his response. Suddenly it struck me that I was now an officer and not some lightweight person using the services of the rest house. Therefore, I duly commanded, 'Get it cleaned again. And please put the mattress in the sun. Meanwhile, I'll have a cup of tea in the garden.'

Having made my first attempt at being officer-like, I trotted to the garden. Fifteen minutes later, there was no sign of the tea or of the room being cleaned. Another ten minutes later I went out in search of Grumpy only to be told that since his shift was over, he was no longer available. His replacement was more pleasant. I got a cup of tea from him, and also an assurance that he'd air the mattress, but along with that several conditions were thrown at me like he'd need help as the mattress was heavy and in any case the sun was to set in another couple of hours and worse still, the monkeys often played havoc with anything put out in the sun. Totally fatigued by then, I stepped out to arm myself with a hand sanitizer, acid to douse the bathroom and some odd rags with Vim powder.

So that was my first day as an OT. Cleaning up someone else's muck and wiping up tears as I felt distinctly morose and very, very alone.

27

'PLEASE, IT'S AN EMERGENCY!'

I woke up next morning to red welts all over my body and cold from allergy; the bed bugs and the carpet dust had done its job. Grumpy was back on duty and I could also spot a sweeper. Upon Ma's advice, I quietly handed the sweeper some money requesting that the carpet and the mattress be aired while I was at work. The sweeper happily pocketed the amount and there and then got down to removing the carpet, which led to another round of sneezing as dust invaded the room. Between sneezes I told him not to place the carpet back in the room and made off to meet my boss.

Obviously, no one can be expected to be in office at 9 a.m. or even at 9:30. I passed time reading random notices around the PA's room. One box, lying at a dangerous tilt on the broken khaki green steel cupboard read 'condom material'. That was intriguing. Material for a health drive to control population perhaps. A sign read 'Cution. Live wire'. The peon and I were thick as thieves by the time my boss strolled in with a cheerful hello and beckoned me to his room. Morning passed with him giving me no indication of what exactly I was expected to do, while I tried coming to grips as what his average day was like. The gent had apparently passed out of a reputed engineering college but gave all signs of being a comfortable bureaucrat with his pot belly and brown clothes. By now I'd figured out that brown in all shades and hues dominated an average bureaucrat's wardrobe.

A few cups of tea later, I went out in search of a loo. When I asked the peon if there was a toilet I could use there was a brief argument between us as he tried to persuade me to use the boss's toilet attached to his room. I couldn't get around to doing that as the door to that was right behind boss's desk and from the sounds of it whatever one did in that loo reverberated outside. Finally, he relented and pointed to the right. I rushed down that way, but could not spot a toilet, just some random three ladies at the end of the passage.

I asked them, 'The toilet please...'

One of the ladies said, 'We don't have toilets.'

I said, 'Excuse me? You don't have any toilets?'

She said, 'No, we don't. We walk across home when we need to go to the toilets.'

Literally bursting I said, 'Please, it's an emergency!'

Then I saw what looked like toilets right across the corridor and rushed to it. I walked in and saw four squat toilets filled with disgusting stuff. I didn't mind that, what I did mind was that none of them had a door. I looked up and down and thought *okay, I have no choice just please god do not let anyone walk in on me*. I went to the last one because I thought that would give me most privacy.

Just as I squatted I heard someone walk in. When I heard the footsteps approaching I looked up to spot a little old man with a walking stick and really thick dark glasses right in front of me, staring. I quickly tried to hold myself because I was about to fall back from the shock. I stared back and was speechless. He however moved to the toilet next to me and took care of his business.

I was genially greeted by my boss who was oblivious to my state of mind when I re-entered his room. He and some other gent were seriously examining a file. Waving it in my direction he said, 'We were just going through something you have asked for.'

Asked for? Me? Apart from demanding a cleaner and more sanitized environment, I had hardly uttered anything to anyone.

'Didn't know that you were in the marriage market. Heh?'

And he guffawed. What marriage market? My perplexed and totally over stressed brain struggled.

'Sir …' I started only to have him rush in with a loud guffaw.

'These fellows have put up a file to me to sanction you a new mate!'

'Ha! Ha! Ha!'

Mate? Me? I grabbed the file from him, all niceties to the wind. There, in neatly typed Times New Roman font size 14 the following words were inscribed: 'Madam Meena Kumari, IAS probationer, has reported for field training in Rishikesh district. She has been allotted Room number 2 in the VIP rest house. She is asking there for a new mate. She is complaining that in her room somewhere there is mating and somewhere there is no mating and somewhere there is dirty mating. Accordingly you may kindly sanction a new mate for her.'

I quietly put the file back on the table, red-faced, feeling totally humiliated. To the credit of the gent however, he figured out my distress and waved away the other guy, called for his car and took me home to join his wife and him for lunch. They made soothing sounds. In fact, his wife invited me to share all their meals with them while I trained in Rishsikesh. My reactions were muted as I pecked at my food. Some signal was obviously shared between the couple and the gent made off elsewhere. Unable to control myself anymore, I simply wept. And wept and wept lots more. I narrated the entire day's events and yesterday's too to her.

Sympathetically she gave me a shoulder to cry on. When the tears ran dry, she said simply, 'Don't get agitated. No one means any harm to you: nothing personal. The people here are good-hearted. It's just that one goes through an initial hump when one joins this service before one can say that one has fully adjusted to it.'

Eyes twinkling, she also clarified that English writing skills were not a strong point in most government offices, and that I would eventually learn to understand a new language altogether, a mixture of Hindi and English far removed from my convent English. This would explain that 'condom' stood for 'condemn' and 'mate' stood for 'mat'!

She was able to pacify me. I confessed to her that this was my first job and also my very first time away from home. I was to take decisions and make choices for myself in an unfamiliar environment. I expressed my fear that I felt lost and all alone at this very point of time.

'Never mind,' she said soothingly, 'I'm here for you. Any time that you face a problem, come to me. Now go wash your face. An officer cannot appear weepy and teary-eyed.'

Mollified and relieved that I seemed to have some sort of a friend in my boss's wife, I returned to work. After lunch, the office seemed to have discarded its somnambulant air. There was a buzz and things were moving. I waded through files familiarizing myself with issues and concepts.

However, by evening it appeared that whatever else I had imagined Indian bureaucracy and the IAS to be, the office routine was fairly pedestrian, terribly unexciting and not at all inspiring.

28

BLAH, BLAH, BLAH!

*B*etween the office and the circuit house the days fell into a pattern. I explored the city a bit but wasn't really into dharmic sthans, which is exactly what Rishsikesh is all about. In any case, I had so far in my life never gone out anywhere sightseeing unless one overlooks my trip to Nainital with Venkat. A couple of times I went out for inspections and field visits, but all in all, nothing great to write home about.

Interestingly, all the government schemes that I'd mugged up for the UPSC exams were now a reality. Frankly, when mugging up for the exam, I had no idea that they'd be mind-numbingly dull routine type of ideas at the ground level requiring huge effort to implement. Someone had said that the disease which inflicts bureaucracy and what bureaucrats usually die from is routine! So true.

One day I entered my boss' room and guess who was sitting there, pretty as a picture? Venkat. Seeing him, in that dull room was an absolute pleasure!

Boss had to push off for a meeting, which left Venkat and me alone for a bit until we opted to move out and sit in the Circuit House garden. As we walked down there was hardly any conversation between us, but yes, my sense of delight in seeing him was obvious. Grumpy, the Circuit House attendant, for once appeared without being yelled for. I ordered for tea and some snacks.

'So,' Venkat asked, 'how are things with you? Are you settled in and enjoying yourself?'

'Well...I can't say that I've settled in. To speak the truth, it's not what I'd expected things would be...I mean the job is not what I'd imagine it.'

'Which was?'

I gave that some serious thought. What had I thought or imagined would be in store when I got through the exam? There had been vague delusions of power and glamour and some sort of thinking that life would become really easy. But that wasn't anything that could be defined as a concrete job expectation, was it? Also, that was not an adequate enough career prospect to tell someone as serious-minded as Venkat, who had probably been guided by a nobler reasoning than mine.

Guess what? I was right. Probably taking my silence as a signal to air his own views on the service Venkat launched into a solid lecture on the joys of the IAS, on how the real India lay in the villages and districts, and how one could turn around a little bit of the country just by being a caring, considerate officer, blah blah blah. It was a long talk that he had warmed up to, and while he rattled on I couldn't help wondering that at some level I could only grudgingly accept his love for his job. Truly motivational. There were few others in the service I had met so far with an iota of Venkat's passion.

That bit over there, was a short silence. Yet, there were several unsaid things between us, many unresolved issues. Possibly both of us thought simultaneously as Venkat started,

'I think... I owe you an apology.'

Almost in real-time I too spoke, 'We need to talk...'

And this was again followed by silence. For whatever reason, the situation appeared funny and we ended up laughing, realizing that there was no need to talk, followed by us heartily tucking away pakodas and chutney made from bhang seeds, a local delicacy. The moment passed and we moved on to general news and gossip of the coaching centre; what Misraji must be up to, and so on and so forth.

As evening dawned and it was time for him to leave, I got despondent, rather apparently. Seeing that, Venkat returned to his lecture mode.

'Don't waste time. This is the only carefree phase in your entire professional life. You should use it carefully. Buy yourself a Kindle,' he said, 'and spend your spare time reading. Roam all over. Do your inspections. Note down things, little things that you'd want to work upon later when you are in an active job.'

I vehemently reacted, 'It's so difficult Venkat. I am all alone; how much can a person do by themselves? I also want to travel and see around but there is no company, and then the inclination to do things by oneself is low.'

There was a short silence and then Venkat quietly uttered, 'It needn't have been so. You need not be or feel alone...'

'Like how?'

'You don't understand what I am saying, do you? That's been your problem. You are always only thinking about yourself. Learn to come to other people's wavelength sometimes. What are you running away from always? Yourself?'

'I am NOT running away.'

'Ask yourself. Only you can answer that. But that's my reading, and believe me, I am a well-wisher and someone who cares deeply for you.'

Just then, it struck me that he'd referred to me as someone who is always only thinking of oneself. I got all hot and bothered and lapsed into a deep sulk.

As the shadows lengthened, we felt a bit distanced, and with a mix of emotions, I walked Venkat to his car and he left.

29

BEING CINDERELLA

*W*asn't Cinderella proof enough that a new pair of shoes can transform your life? So, I too decided to tweak changes in mine. For a start, I got into a fitness mode and resumed running. On the office front, instead of treating everything as a wretched waste of time, I began making regular records in my diary. I'd suppose that like me there would have been countless probationers to have come and gone from this dreary Circuit House who by now would be hale and hearty seniors in my service. They'd have survived, which was reason enough to believe that I too would. Seriously, what was it that was bothering me? Home was close by; I was in a premier job and had been allotted a decent state. Work on the positives is what I repeated to myself as a mantra.

The boss also noted my changed demeanor and would crack jokes, some really inappropriate ones; it must have been a relief for him to have a happy trainee.

In any case, when we are dispatched to our respective districts, we are given a very rigorous schedule and countless assignments. Ideally, I should have stuck to those schedules and finished the work. But now it had been almost a month and I was far away from starting on them. One project was barely finished when boss announced that the chief minister was to visit our district, which meant that all things were to put on hold; we tried putting things together at a frenetic pace ahead of the visit.

We kept track of the chief minister's visit to the previous district and learnt to our worry that it had not been a happy scene there. He had inspected the district hospital, and seeing the poor hygiene, suspended its chief medical superintendent. In the adjoining districts two lower-level officials were removed. The saga went on.

It was my first exposure to political bosses. I only had the irksome memories of Baba, and his continuous run-in with the district bosses. The thought of being ticked off was frightening, a full-fledged failure which might invoke something more than a censure. Even boss was on edge, and we spent long hours at work, both in the office as well as in the field. I felt bad for the suspended chief medical superintendent, as the thought that this could well have been Baba crossed my mind.

However, things went off well, extremely well. Boss also turned out to be an astute manager. I saw a different side of him: gone was the cheerful, happy laid back person. In his place was a self-effacing, boot-licking individual whose every sentence was peppered with 'Ji haan, Sir! Jaroor ho jaiga!' (Yes, Sir, it will be done). His assistant informed us that boss's wife had gone off with Mrs Chief Minister to do some temple sighting and shopping. And did I not know that the chief minister's daughter, shortly to get married, was assisted in sartorial choices by none other than the boss's wife! Wheels within wheels, all this made for a benevolent inspection, some fulsome praises of our work, and lots of all round cheer and happiness.

I was introduced to the chief minister, who gave me a once over, made some indifferent noises welcoming me to the state, and thereafter dismissing me, all in a span of a minute.

'Inse sikhiye, kaam karna (Learn from your boss),' he instructed, pointing to my boss.

With my respect for the man, my boss, at nadir point, I agitatedly thought, sure I would, over my dead body. But phew! One huge experience was under the belt.

Later at the dinner, where the women sat separate from the men, boss's wife was tittering all over the place in full attendance of Mrs Chief Minister. Frankly, Mrs Chief Minister looked simple, like someone who had emerged from the rustic interior. But our chief minister is our chief minister, and so we had a full display of Mrs Boss' 'how-to-appease-Mrs Chief Minister–skills'. I sat far away, quietly observing the husband-wife duo at work, thinking how on earth I would handle such situations later in my career.

But luck eluded me; I was beckoned to meet Mrs Chief Minister.

'Madam!' gushed Mrs Boss at Mrs Chief Minister, 'Yeh hamari sabse nanhi bachchi hai (This is one of our young entrants into the IAS). She is really scared and raw. So, I have been mentoring her.'

Like hell man! I am definitely not anyone's child, and took umbrage at being mentored by someone's wife. Before any further comments could be made about me, I hastily informed Mrs Chief Minister that I was an IAS probationer on training. Boss's wife ruthlessly overruled my low toned intervention and continued to inform Mrs Chief Minister that I was a delight to have in the district, and that anytime Mrs Chief Minister so desired, I could be available for her shopping, temple hopping and general company.

My jaw dropped. Hello! What was all this about? I refused to jump with joy at the offer. The boss's wife hissed at me that I was letting a golden opportunity go, that this encounter could cost me my future in the state. Really?! A terrible rage built up inside me. Who on earth was she to tell me how to plan or manage my career? So I was curt and decidedly impolite in my response that whatever be my future, chumming up to the wife of a chief minister was best left to the likes of wives of IAS officers. To compound matters, I firmly ended that I was an officer first and a woman next, and that the two roles should not be confused. Mrs Chief Minister heard most of this conversation, probably took an instant aversion to me, which was good enough to terminate the beginnings of any relationship between us.

Then I made for the Circuit House, abandoning the dinner, the chief minister, Mrs Chief Minister and whosoever else was a part of the gathering.

30

JEKYLL AND HYDE TYPE OF AVATAR

Despondent and feeling the desperate need to talk to someone, I called home. Baba was of little help. He first got into a total state that I had argued with my seniors, then panicked and finally counselled that the foremost thing I should do the next morning is to ease out things with my boss' wife. In fact, he advised that I go across to the chief minister's place of stay too and make amends. Like hell I'll do that Baba, I thought, and nearly banged the phone on him. Seconds later, Ma called. She sounded worried sick, as if the world had come to an end. Then Bhai called, duly prodded by Baba, and by then I was so fed up that I switched off the phone and tried to get some sleep.

I spent a restless night clouded with nightmares! Somewhere in the nightmares lurked my boss who was constantly wagging his finger at me. So I woke up less rested and more stressed. It didn't help that the mobile carried several missed calls from my parents and SMSes too.

Grumpy also seemed to have a different look that morning. In fact, he hovered around while I listlessly poked at my breakfast. Then, he probably lost total self-control. He asked

me about last night's dinner. Okay was my short response.
Huh? He responded, but had I not returned early? The dinner
had finished only in the wee hours of the morning. I chose to
ignore that. But what I couldn't ignore was his natter that the
boss' wife is actually hard as nails and wears the pants in the
house. I gave him a really cold look and made off for my room.

I tried evaluating the situation. What had happened
last night between me and the madam boss and Mrs Chief
Minister may have been of little consequence in a large metro.
But in a town like Rishikesh it was definitely BIG news. I
could have perhaps controlled myself better, but what the
heck; I was fatigued running around getting my district in
order for this visit, and just when I thought that the inspection
was over and I could chill a bit, someone decided to dump
this whole 'priya sakhi' type of stuff on me, a Jekyll and Hyde
type of avatar, where I play officer part-time and simpering
woman otherwise.

I called Venkat. Not that I wanted to, but I was honestly
totally frazzled and it was not even nine o' clock yet. My ego
said not to call, but then who else do I turn to at this point
of time? My family, my only support, has no understanding of
bureaucracy. I have no friends from the training academy whom
I could trust with this incident, and there was no one else I
could turn to either for advice. So I decided that I'd give his
mobile one ring. If he responded then it was destined that I
take his advice on this mess or else I figure it out on my own.

Well, one ring and pronto, Venkat responded. 'Hi! What
makes you call me this time in the morning?'

'I think I'm in trouble Venkat...,' I muttered, and then
launched into a narrative of the entire encounter of the previous
night.

There was silence from the other end, followed by an amused query, 'So you ticked all of them?'

'Yes I did. And I now feel that the whole place is going to treat me as if I'm afflicted by the plague. Not that I'm bothered, but still. Why on earth should I suck up to a chief minister's wife? I mean, am I not an officer and not an officer's wife? How can the two roles be confused? And even if I were merely an officer's wife, do you think that I'd have the skills to shop and suck up as was expected from me? After all ...'

'You did well,' interjected Venkat, 'you did well.'

Relief gushed out of me like water from a blocked drain. I started to feel that I'd blown the event out of proportion. Whatever the tension that was had dissipated, and ratification that my impromptu and natural response had been correct, from someone who was my senior and a die hard bureaucrat, was sheer relief. Venkat sensed that I was upset and continued to give me some more placebo type of relief. He described bureaucrats to be of various sorts, and the sort which made a career of being a servile doormat to the top hierarchy through their wives was the worst. What I could figure out was that this sort was common and not his type, but at the end of the day there was enough space in bureaucracy to accommodate all types.

'Be yourself. Go to office. By tomorrow this will be past. I know there will be some tension between your boss and you, but don't forget that maybe he too will be carrying a guilt that his wife tried bullying you.'

With these comforting words, he said he had to push off for some meeting. Extremely relieved, I left for work, deciding that after hanging around at the place for an hour or so, I'd head for a field inspection. That way, the boss and I wouldn't have much time with each other. We'd be giving each other some space.

Well, I needn't have worried. Boss didn't turn up and wasn't even expected until lunch. So I did my bit of work and decided to visit a neighbouring district where another batchmate was training. That'd give me a break.

31

DARPOK! DARPOK!

There was a lovely place on the way to Tehri from Rishikesh where one could spot the river turning on a bend. It had only lush green undergrowth and was dotted sparsely with goatherds and their flock. The car stopped there for a bit. I walked down towards the river bed, away from the gaze of my driver. Flinging my arms in the air I whirled and whirled and whirled. The light breeze, the strong sun and the cold air was miraculous. The boys with the goats were laughing at the sight of me! Grinning back, I gave away my sandwiches to them and climbed up and back into the car to resume my journey.

Throughout the ride though, I felt shackled into the facade of being an officer. Frankly, I wished to hop into one of the Garhwal buses hiccuping past, full of people, children and the odd goats. To be really free, I thought, one needs to be away from the trappings of bureaucracy. Yes, I think at that point of time, I really hated bureaucracy and the fact that I was not a free person.

Then my mobile went ping and an SMS from Venkat read, 'Sorted?'

'Yes, thanks,' I responded. 'I bothered you unnecessarily.'

'Always there for you. I would have come across, but things are tight here.'

Gosh, this guy was like my family! They never leave me alone. But he had been of great help, so I politely responded that he needn't bother, and that in any case I was not in Rishikesh but was on my way to meet a batchmate in Tehri.

The signal dropped as the car entered Tehri. Was I glad to meet my batchmate? Can't say, really. We had been part of the group which had hung out at night, and this guy was a master at the art of cutting classes. He was bindaas and seemingly good, harmless fun.

We chatted until night set in. In the parts around here, dinner was an early meal, after which we sat out in the Circuit House verandah and watched the fireflies against the shadows of the trees. A little later my colleague excused himself, only to return with a bottle and two glasses.

'Whiskey,' he announced. 'Let's have a drink.'

I was taken aback. I am not much of a drinker though occasionally I had been party to his gang which drank at the academy. But the mood was such that I didn't say no and found myself with a glass in hand. Maybe, I thought, when he was not looking, I would pour it out. So I sat nursing my drink, tipping it out now and then when he was not looking. Several glasses down the guy was a riot. He was regaling me with hilarious tales of his district experiences which had me in splits. Some of the encounters were downright vulgar but what the heck! After long I was relaxed and enjoying myself.

'Not getting hooked?' he asked all of a sudden.

'Who me…?' I spluttered, taken aback.

'Who else? You know what? In the academy we called you the not-marrying type. Amongst the guys we'd quiz whether you were engaged or in a relationship or whether you were just waiting for a miracle in your life. Attractive as you are, you have got a sharp tongue and a lousy demeanour, don't you, honey? Scared shit of you, that's us men. Ha! Ha! Ha!'

I should have retreated to my room and called it a night as I was seriously offended, but I am a sucker and a fool. I hung around trying to justify to him that I was a marrying type, and this and that.

'Well,' he interrupted, 'if you are the marrying type then don't look at me. I'm already hooked. But of course, I can give you a couple of quick lessons on how to keep your man happy in bed.'

I could smell his breath really close by now and was scared shit. This guy had totally lost it. There was no foreseeing what he would do. So I edged away and then ran to my room. He was close at my heels trying to grab me.

The night passed with him banging at my door shouting, 'Open up! Open up! Darpok! Darpok!'

At times he'd shout, 'Come on darling, come out for a hug. Just a hug, I promise.'

Gosh, the situation had got out of hand and it was all my doing. Shouldn't I have lashed back at him when he'd called me a conformed spinster and commented at my poor personality? Too late now.

At the crack of dawn, by which time this drama had stopped, I peeped out to find this guy sprawled on a chair with the bottles and glasses littered on the grass. What would the staff think when they reported for duty? I removed the signs of last night's revelry and deposited them in my suitcase as I tiptoed out. I'd dispose these somewhere en route I reckoned. I called the driver, and as quick as I could, we were on the road, back to Rishikesh. I was traumatized. When we passed that beautiful spot on the river bend again, it just didn't look as appealing. By now worry was killing me; the events of last night would be the news of Uttarakhand. Surely, between the two incidents, would my reputation not be sullied beyond repair? In one, I had appeared rude and upset my seniors, while in the other, I had had a drunk batchmate grab for me. And then, how would I dispose of the bottles? The moment Grumpy would take the case out of the car, they'd rattle. I couldn't just dump them in the Circuit House bin, could I? That would then set off rumors that I was a closet drinker to boot!

Totally immersed in this seemingly hopeless situation, I was taken aback when the driver cleared his throat and said, 'Madam, may I say something?'

'Bolo,' I said.

'The sir we went to visit is drunk all the time. It is his normal behaviour...'

I caught the driver's eye in the rearview mirror. It looked sympathetic and concerned. There was nothing to say in response. However, when we stopped for a bite, I handed him the bottles wordlessly for disposal.

Reaching Rishikesh, I was definitely more mature and hugely discouraged. There was never a moment that I was truly enjoying being an IAS officer. Honestly, everything about it sucked. I sent a short SMS to my sounding board Venkat, 'How, just how do you enjoy this lousy service and keep yourself going? The people suck. The working sucks. The bosses suck...'

'Now what? What happened?'

I didn't reply; he sent another SMS which read, 'take a break and go home.'

Which was the best advice I'd ever got. So I took leave and boarded the next train for Bareilly.

32

SHOPPING!

*M*a and Baba went out of their way to brighten up my stay. Dussehra was round the corner so the atmosphere was vibrant. My room was done up with new linen and a mellow lamp. Various celebrations and outings were lined up, including one at the Bareilly Club. Carrying the shame of the last two incidents at work, I made an effort to join in the festive spirit and camouflage my unease on the work front. I fasted with Ma and indulged in all the vrat ka khana, the special food eaten while fasting. In fact, it was interesting to discover how it was cooked. A fleeting thought of starting a food blog instead of struggling with bureaucracy did come to my mind, but the moment passed as I tucked in the fare.

We met up with various relatives. Bua was in town with her sneaky style of probing about my marriage plans. That apart, the holiday was turning out to be a refreshing break.

On the second day, Ma asked if I had enough money with me, and how I was handling my finances. By now I was almost eight months into the job and the thought of discussing my earnings with my parents had not even crossed my mind. Has Bua said something to Ma?

'Do you need money, Ma?' I asked, after a long silence in which I battled with guilt, shame and sheer remorse.

I was pretty aware what it must have taken tremendous effort on Ma's part to even raise the issue, and I was sheepish about it.

'No. No. Nothing like that. Just that your Baba was mentioning that you have visited us twice since you got the job, but each time we find that you haven't talked about this at all, and your Bua was also wondering how much you earned and...'

Oops! I thought. How stupid of me. This should have been discussed between us. Moreover, with my first earnings I should have bought Baba a new shirt, got Ma a new sari, given Jojo a new collar and maybe taken care of the little details in the house. Where was the difference between Bhai and me? Once we were financially independent, both of us had never given a part of our salaries with our parents. Trust that nosy parker aunt of mine to drive the point in and make Ma feel terrible.

With a quick comeback I told Ma that I had planned a surprise sari shopping for her that afternoon. Her face beamed. I felt really small when she said that she could now boast at the club that the sari she was wearing had been bought by her IAS daughter.

All said and done, it was a lovely shopping expedition and I ensured that Ma bought the sari she wanted, regardless of the cost. For Baba, we got a fancy kurta, and feeling indulgent, I even bought Ma a small pair of gold ear studs, and also a sari for Bua. At the family do that night, my parents glowed and were complimented profusely by our relatives. I was pleased to see that, but still, my mind was partly occupied with the terrible thought that once this mindless stuff was over, I would need to report back for training to a hostile boss and a co-officer who had tried to force himself on me.

I was neither happy nor relaxed, and the memory of the IAS results was the only bit of ecstasy that I could recall in recent times. The academy sucked, my colleagues were ratty and time hung on my hands after those years of slog and study. But my problems were trivial. There was great family joy that there was an IAS officer in their midst.

A little later, I went to the house and sat on the steps gazing at nothing, sitting tight with my sense of disconnect with the sounds of joy and merriment wafting outside.

33

ATTRACTING UNDUE ATTRACTION

*L*uckily, the return to Rishikesh was not so bad. All those assignments required to be submitted at the academy had to be wrapped up, which kept me gainfully occupied. Boss was distant but pleasant. With just 3–4 weeks to go, I could avoid his wife and just be busy. Things would have continued like this but for an unpleasant call that I received from a colleague.

'Hey! Have you been fighting with your boss?'

'No,' I responded.

'Well, I am already at the academy and it is the talk here. In fact, the CD also told me that you had some problem with another trainee, that you had gone to spend a weekend with him and…'

'Look, I don't know where this story has come from,' I firmly replied, and hung up.

So, I guess, things would haunt me. On the one hand, I felt like telling my batchmate that, for all of you who gossip about me, thanks for making me the centre of your world! But realistically speaking, in each batch there are the types who are pilloried for one thing or another. With these two incidents, there was a good chance that I would be the one to be at the receiving end of the possible ridicule. With a heavy heart, I packed up and left for Mussoorie.

It took time, but eventually I managed to make peace with the circumstances. For one, I had been allotted a single room. Next, I made it a point to sit in the dining hall, at times by myself. I began participating in lectures. There was no point in sitting around, asking, 'Oh no, what am I going to do.' It was best to behave as if nothing had happened at all.

You know what, it worked! Yes! After a while, even with my sense of isolation, more interesting bits of gossip took over. Like who had ditched who, who had had got more dowry and who spent their training period scouting for CBM, etc. In any case, just as luck would have it, one of our bachelor professors, on deputation from his home state, fell hopelessly in love with a batchmate of mine. The girl was someone whom no one liked and was really one of the more ghastly looking specimens of our batch, but as they popular saying goes: when you are in love then you are in love. Here, love became the rallying point of all gossip. There'd be daily bulletins on the ever-expanding romance and it helped that the girl was caught a couple of times sneaking out from the prof's residence at early hours. Yet again, destiny came to my rescue. My teeny tiny issues were relegated to the back burner.

34

RED SPELLS DANGER

The last lap of training saw most of us in different phases of our lives with differing thinking. Some married, some ruing their cadres, but most of the batchmates happy in their avatars as IAS officers.

There is a Gender Studies cell in the academy. We'd heard that a new officer had been appointed to head it and guess what?! It was none other than Leela whom I'd met in Venkat's office. Her chiffon, perfume and red nail enamel were intact! Obviously, she had by now discarded her disdain for working at the academy! The other surprise was that she instantly recognized me as I passed by her in the dining room.

'You know the lady?' asked my companion.

'I've met her just once in another officer's room at Bareilly.'

'That one is really a colourful piece', was the unwarranted information. 'Her father was in the Indian Foreign Service and she has mostly studied abroad. She qualified for the IAS in the first attempt and never misses an opportunity to display her international upbringing.'

And so he went blah blah. I gave him half an ear until I heard him utter Venkat's name. That's when my ears jerked.

'You know, in her batch the lone person she thought was up to her standard was some Andhra fellow called Venkat. She'd hang out with him alone and everyone thought that the two of them would get married. She would sit next to him, travel with him and they both are in the same state too. It's a bit of surprise that she has come to the academy on a posting.'

'Why surprise?' I asked

'Because Venkat is not here!'

And the fellow erupted into laughter as though he had cracked the joke of his lifetime.

I shouldn't have been affected but I was. Really, I was. I mean I knew that they were close, Venkat and this dame, but a romance between them? No, no, no. Not possible. In my room I turned restless. I had no inkling that this could have been a possibility. But why should this affect me so much? After all, I had been avoiding any close relationship with Venkat. But well, I was disturbed and spent a restless night. When I did manage to get sleep, the lady appeared in my dreams tossing her head back and delicately laughing. Venkat was holding her hand and heading with her towards a misty spot. Were my dreams trying to tell me something?

Next morning, the first class was on Gender Studies. After my disturbing night I decided to skip it. Luck was not on my side though. I soon bumped into the lady. She looked pretty tensed about something, but there was no way that I could've avoided her, so I wished her, 'Morning Ma'am.'

'Where were you in the morning? Why are you bunking classes? I lamely replied that I had overslept. But this wasn't enough. She was livid and said that she will take it up with the course director and that probably I'd have to see him. Well, I was shaken up rather severely.

Later, I got to know that the very first class she had taken had been rough for her. She had begun on a wrong note by announcing: 'No cell phones in class please! No texting as well. I'll know what you are doing when you look down at your crotch and smile!'

Thereafter she had promptly gone ahead to take a longish call herself on her cell phone. She was ill-prepared, messed up concepts and spoke utter nonsense. Maybe it was the lack of experience, but the class was ruthless in making her feel that she was raw. My luck was such that I walked into her just after this and got the rough end of the stick.

After class I was summoned by her to the course director's room. Normally the guy was pretty cool and chilled out, but I thought him to be out of depth today when confronted by a hysterical lady with red nails and chiffon. He sort of tried brokering peace between us but eventually gave in to the lady. I had to accordingly take leave for the day. Boy, was I miffed? Seething with rage at the unfairness of it all, and having already lost half a holiday, I decided to go off for a long walk towards the Tibetan settlement beyond the academy.

That was a good thing to do. We had been so bound down by the academy routine that enjoying the local area had been the lowest on our priority. A long walk downhill led me to the Tibetan settlements, a Tibetan monastery and several red-cheeked, happy-looking children and adults. I sat in a local dhaba and ate thukpa and adventurously ordered rice beer, which was so mind altering that the steep uphill climb back didn't trouble me a mite.

Must do that again, I thought, as I turned in for the night. I also hoped that tonight my dreams would be of Tibetan food and rice beer instead of Venkat's ex-girlfriend. However, whatever lay in the future for us, the battle lines between the lady and me were clearly drawn, and being on the weaker side, I needed to watch my step.

35

FAULT IN MY STARS

*A*ctually, it was Sweety who put the thought in my head. One evening, while we were chatting, she started on how she had visited an astrologer to find out when she would bear a child, that too, only a male child. I was listening to her with half an ear but later it struck me that perhaps I should too visit an astrologer, because really, the last few weeks had been pretty unnerving with life throwing one shit after another at me.

I tentatively broached the issue with a batchmate who turned all serious and informed me that we live in a world where there is a lot of pressure for everything to be mainstream, where you have to be 'civilized, predictable, obedient and normal'. But life does not care about all that. Reality does not always behave in the way that present day science dictates. Therefore? Therefore, for answers one must trust mystics. And so it was. Here, let me make my stand very clear. As much as I want to believe that I have no faith in astrology and that none of my decisions would be influenced by it, I concede otherwise. After all, I was what I am because of Baba's faith in astrology. Sometimes I think that I have gotten myself into seriously dangerous situations by being too naive and trusting, and yet got out of them. Was it my stars protecting me? Also, I realized of late that I was rather incapable of running my life. How on earth would I manage the future? I was looking for all these answers in my stars.

It turned out that Mussoorie had a reputed astrologer. So one day my batchmate and I made our way to the place; she because she wanted to know if her CBM would work out and me for sheer consolation.

The astrologer was a lady clothed in black. We sat on two rickety chairs in a tiny room. I awaited my turn as the astrologer turned to my batchmate first. The batchmate and the astrologer discussed in detail the various ups and downs in her love life. The batchmate was consoled particularly when she was told that she'd face better times from the month of February.

My turn now. We started on the routine stuff, personality, career, etc., and then the astrologer abruptly said, 'Now let's talk about relationships.' I froze. She continued. Apparently I have some an astral configuration that prevents me from getting close to people and makes me extremely self-centred and also inward-looking. But seemingly, at this very point of time, I have the chance of love, and that too only for a limited period of time, which I should grab else I'll be alone all my life. And, of course, I should be wary of enemies who are constantly trying to damage me. That was all the astrologer was willing to say.

The batchmate and I returned without an exchange of words, each wrapped in our prospective fates and future. I needed to work fast or else be confined to a life of permanent spinsterhood. Surely, I couldn't die a virgin? A worse thought. And where on earth would I find a man to wed and bed immediately? I had not even considered any of my batchmates as being worthy of a second look, and it was really too late to start making eyes at them when probation was close to finishing. As it were, they weren't really viewing me as a 'someone-who-wanted-to-marry' type.

The evening gloom had set in, the way it can only in a hill station, and it was with a heavy heart and sickening feeling that I hit the sack. Damn that astrologer and damn Sweety for giving me that idea to visit her and damn life for putting me through this. It's not as though I had not been dreaming of a Prince Charming in my life. I've been there, done that for close to a decade to no avail.

At night, as sleep deluded me, I finally concluded that it was Baba and his stupid ambition that had brought this state of affairs on me. Had he not nursed an IAS dream for me, I would've charted a different path and maybe been a happier person.

36

FINALLY, I COMMIT

The only man who had shown a worthy interest in me resurfaced in my life the very next day. Venkat was in the academy for a lecture. He'd messaged in advance, but wary of Leela I avoided fixing any programme until he would be free and call himself. He did call and we decided to meet up at a café outside the campus.

Venkat was late and accompanied by Leela which like put me off totally. Surely, he must have been aware that things between us were not good and, in any case, what she had done to me was pretty much unbearable. What gave me a deep sense of satisfaction was that she was as uncomfortable as me, while Venkat was oblivious to any of the undercurrents. We chatted about this and that and predictably much of the conversation moved in directions that excluded me totally. But after a while, Leela had to move off for elsewhere, which let the two of us alone. So we ordered another round of coffee and Venkat said, 'So, tell me what you are up to?'

'Nothing much. Just this and that.'

'Your this and that is always interesting, so tell me.'

'Well, for one, I am daggers drawn with this friend of

yours. She is a royal, nasty piece of shit!'

And Venkat laughed uproariously at that. To my surprise, he leaned across and whispered conspiratorially, 'Shall I let you into a secret? We nearly got married...'

'What?!' I exclaimed.

He was being so upfront about it.

'Yeah, but somehow I couldn't imagine spending my life with her.'

Then, grinning wickedly, he asked, 'Her perfume is overwhelming, isn't it? Not to talk of the red nails...'

I was stunned; Venkat was being very bitchy. Both of us convulsed into laughter.

'However, you have to get married one day Venkat, don't you?' I asked.

'Well, the girl I wanted to marry wasn't ready for me or marriage.'

'Which girl will say no to you, Venkat? You are a paragon of virtues.'

Help! Was I flirting with this guy?

'Will you marry me if I asked?'

Silence, a long silence. Then the image of the astrologer reared up in my mind, and so I simply said, 'Ask me and you won't find me wanting.'

He relaxed, called for the waiter, paid the bill and hustled me out to a lonely nook of Mussoorie where we grabbed for each other and kissed and kissed and kissed until we were gasping for breath.

'You are one really difficult girl. How long you have made me wait,' Venkat muttered in my ear, part nibbling at it, part talking.

There was nothing to talk, really, so I silenced him with a kiss.

Venkat was putting up at a place slightly away from the academy and we made our way there. This time, there were no reservations on his side that we wait for marriage or some such shit. Well, I lost my virginity. I was relieved that the astrologer had made me think straight at least on that front.

37

FALLING IN LOVE

I woke up next morning to the feel of something gentle over my face. A delicious warm sunlight, its first rays greeted me as I opened my eyes. Venkat was gently running his hand over my face as if in wonderment that I was there, with him. He smiled. I think there and then, and the astrologer be damned, I fell hopelessly in love. Totally embarrassed by this realization, my discordant first words to him after that wondrous night were, 'Who drew the curtains? I hate sunlight. I mean...'

Venkat, softly said, 'Ssshh, don't say anything. I love you. In fact, I love thee with the breath, smiles and tears of all my life, and if god choose, I shall but love thee better after death.'

I swallowed, totally wordless.

'Not my words. Elizabeth Barrett Browning wrote these in a sonnet for her husband.'

There was nothing to say. Don't know poetry in any case, and English literature never fascinated me, but his words were so beautiful that I was overwhelmed with love and a longing to be back in his arms.

But I had no such luck. Obviously, both of us had to part really early, he for his workplace and me for the academy. We also had to get away before anyone spotted us. So I left in a rush, taking the three-kilometre-walk to my room and praying that the early morning joggers would not spot me sneaking back into the hostel.

It is a wondrous feeling to be in love. And be sure that I was, actually, in love. I think I had finally found some sort of an anchoring emotion which was mine and mine alone. It had taken a while for me to recognize it, but well, as they say, better late than never.

Venkat had told me that we'd talk at length later in the day, and had asked me to keep quiet about things until then. Well, I guess he knew better; in any case, he was the one who had recognized our love which, like 'duh', I had taken all this while to concede.

I flew to my room, walked in a daze to class and probably had a beatific smile on my face. Several people commented that I looked different. Of course, I would look different. I recommend love and a good dose of sex to look and feel different. Inevitably, as usual, the first class was on Gender Studies to be taken by Leela. But I could now tolerate her. After all, in the undrawn battle lines between us, had I not won the battle and the war, et al.?

Later in the day Venkat and I chatted. After the initial love talk in which I ended up breaking an emotional barrier in me, I told him that I wanted him back physically, with me instead of some hundreds of kilometres away. He asked me how we go about things. Why ask me was my simple response. He could do whatever he wished. I only wanted to be with him.

'Your parents?' he queried. 'How would they respond to the situation?'

'What situation?' I queried.

'About us being a pair, what else?!'

Well how could I tell him that they'd been egging me on in any case to become a pair with him? So actually the reaction would be more of 'finally they've done it' rather than of surprise or shock.

But Venkat was a principled man. He pushed off to Bareilly and went to meet my parents.

'Meena and I wish to marry,' he told them.

To give credit to them, Ma and Baba beautifully hid their emotions of ecstasy and sheer delight. He told them that he had also discussed this with his family and that there was no issue. He informed them that we would try and get married as soon as possible.

Of course, he didn't tell me that he had made this little trip, which resulted in our very first quarrel of a gargantuan proportion. I think the entire hostel would have heard me scream into the phone. But at the end of the day, I feel that Venkat knows me better than I do myself. He simply asked me, 'What exactly is your problem? I mean what's your issue with my formally broaching the issue with your parents?'

'Why don't you realize, Venkat? They'll feel offended that you told them instead of me? After all, I am their child, not you…'

Upon which, after a longish silence, Venkat just terminated the call by saying that he saw no issue in this whole thing and that I needed to sort out my mind first.

I dreaded talking with my parents, but Venkat was right. Things fell into place. Only Sweety raised the discordant note, when she mischievously told me on the phone that I'd been acting too coy about this whole thing from the very beginning, and that she knew we'd end up a couple.

Actually, if I got down to analyze my emotions, it was sheer embarrassment that I felt on having to face my parents. I mean like how do I transit from being a girl to a woman with them? Further, the relationship disclosure would raise questions about when we would marry. And I found getting married and the hoopla surrounding that to be very embarrassing too. All the people likely to tell me what to expect and what to do was an irritating thought. I don't like the ceremonies associated with weddings—the sangeet, the mehendi, haldi ki rasam, the games. Don't get me wrong, I am grateful that I have people who would want to celebrate and rejoice in my marriage, but it is just so awkward. And then, everyone would know that Venkat and I would have sex which would really freak me out.

Maybe, I thought, we should consider a kind of a quiet wedding in Coonoor, where the chances of the Bareilly-wallahs landing up to celebrate would be dim.

38

BE A ROBIN HOOD?

*I*n no time the training period was to draw to a close. I was relieved and probably feeling more stable now that I was in a committed relationship. There was, however, a niggling doubt. In real life, I had started to feel, long distance relationships don't work. One lives in a world of fantasy in such a situation. I mean, there is passion, intensity and loving, but can such a relationship be treated as battle-tested? So, I raised this issue with Venkat. I told him that I felt that romantic relationships require commitment, touch with reality, but most of all they require action because the majority of the time spent together in long distance relationships is precious.

'Nope,' was his short response.

'What do you mean "nope"? Don't you think that long distance relationships usually exist in a suspended "honeymoon state", where everything is nice and happy but devoid of the reality that is necessary to determine if the relationship will ultimately sink or swim?'

'Are you writing some PhD?' was Venkat's prompt counter. 'Please respond to emotion and not thought. This is not a theory paper in some Sociology exam that you need to work out a matrix and a response and logic.'

Well this long distance relationship, in which I had entered, could be pretty much be just a 'honeymoon' at a distance. We needed to be back together and soon. Or so I thought.

As compensation we'd try and communicate often. Even though we were miles apart, technology connected our hearts: through SMSes, through emails, and whatever. But, but, but, there were times when maintaining communication became difficult, probably because either of us was busier than the other at any given point of time. Normally, if I was the busy one, I'd warn Venkat by sending a quick email or text, or a brief phone call. No such luck from him though. If busy, he'd just not respond to my call. Nor had he visited the academy again. I guess he was tied up will all sorts of things; after all he was posted in the Chief Minister's district. But tab bhi, you can't block and unblock a person as though it were an option on the phone.

However, time was running out at the academy for us. We were to move on to functional jobs shortly, and we were being exposed to a spate of talks on what to expect in our postings. Without doubt, all the speakers were passionate about their jobs; being an IAS officer seemed to be some sort of a highlight in their lives. For example, this person, who came in to talk to us about her first posting in one of the most backward districts in her state spoke down to us in a fairly didactic manner aka 'You know when I reported to my district I found that physical and human infrastructure was majorly lacking. I was really blessed and fortunate to get a district like this for my first posting because you know what, everywhere you see, there is *so much* opportunity to do something great and wonderful.'

Some backbenchers sniggered, amused by the lady with her

bouncy hair and chatty style. They also sensed an unwitting prey; one of them raised his hand to ask, 'So, Madam, what did you do there to better the place?'

'I am so glad you asked this,' she said, 'I would like to recount just one experience. After joining my district, I inspected a Block Resource Centre where training of teachers was going on. As expected, most teachers were absent. I took immediate action against them, and guess what happened?'

'What happened, Ma'am?' asked the backbencher.

'The people started shouting slogans in my praise "ziladhikari zindabad". I felt humbled to my core because these people have such low expectations from administration that even the most mundane thing I would do here would be huge for them. I hope I am able to do some good work in my new place of posting as well. Wish me luck guys!'

'All the best, Ma'am!' we chorused.

One really mocking type even expressed his sincere hope that he visit her district to see its bettered and improved version.

Another guest officer, a retired ex-bureaucrat, gave us a different perspective. 'You know,' he said, 'civil servants are bureaucrats who often significantly influence decision making of the government. However, the average day of an IAS officer looks very much like any other bureaucrat's day. A daily schedule might include checking mails, meetings with superiors, chairing meetings, attending business lunches, file work, attending a meeting, answering letters/mail, filing, and finally you can call it a day unless there is an emergency...'

Sounded rotten to me. What a way to spend your day.

'So, Sir, what makes this job so different from the others? I mean what makes us different from other services?' asked another backbencher.

Most people had figured out by now that one takes risks with guest speakers only from the states other than the ones allotted to them for fear of future, so accordingly the insolence levels varied. Our guest puffed up his chest like a penguin, and launched into a discourse on the virtues of being an IAS officer.

'Let me tell you first and foremost the facilities and perks provided to an IAS officer. You get free electricity and telephone. While on tour you get accommodation in very good government bungalows and rest houses. Imagine, after 2 to 4 years in a service you can apply for study leave in a reputed foreign university, the cost of which will be paid by the government. Your salary gets doubled after seven to nine years. And you can get security guards, gardeners, servants and cooks.'

We sniggered, really sniggered hard. This was the pits. I'd be sitting in a remote area of Uttarakhand with free electricity and phone and a huge house and security guards. And doing what with them?!

'Sir,' a trainee officer asked, 'but what about facilitating change within the organization? How does one go about that? The bureaucracy as an organization is under attack. It is now a tool of political leadership. We are an extremely qualified generation of officers who can be used as a talent pool for changing the face of the nation ...'

'Set up an NGO if you want to change the nation. Become an outsider to the system. Educate people as much as you can. Fight for their rights. Help them become self-sufficient and not dependent on the government. Look, no one changed the system by being within it. Leave the system if you want to be an agent of change ...'

'No, Sir, what I meant was ...'

'You meant nothing. Most of you are too young to know

what you want from life. The process you undergo in the initial years of posting is like the weathering of a rock. You learn the system and how the limited change you can make is in ensuring that policies and programmes are properly implemented. Learn to stay with the villagers now and then to know how to eliminate the levels of bureaucracy and corruption that prevent them from becoming the true beneficiaries of government schemes. Get rid of your car with the red beacon. Be the change you want to see.'

He had got our attention. This was a mix of cynicism and advocacy we were hearing. Before we could assimilate our thoughts, he said the final words, slowly, and in a low tone. 'Finally, be a Robin Hood. Rob the rich and maybe become corrupt (there is no other way to survive), but donate all money to the poor.'

Horrified, our CD rushed in to seal the session and thanked the speaker. It certainly was not what the academy had wanted us to imbibe. Nevertheless, unwittingly, we had received a counter-view, a different way of thinking.

The session closed with most of us lost in our thoughts. What would we do? Be a rubber stamp? Become Robin Hood? Live as a person who gets thrown around ever so often? Is that what the future held for most of us? Why on earth did we travel on this road? We are a generation raised on new ideas and new professional opportunities. Why this then?

39

A SURPRISE PACKAGE!

*U*ttarakhand, here I come! But before that, a visit to Venkat's family at Coonoor. Venkat insisted that I join him there as he was holidaying with his family. Unconventional as it were, my parents had no choice but to relent, now that more or less we were engaged to get married. There were no direct flights or trains or buses between New Delhi to Coonoor. The convenient and fastest way to reach there was to take a flight from New Delhi to Coimbatore and then hire a taxi from there. So poorer by ₹20,000, I made way to the place. Coonoor turned out to be a beautiful place despite my disinclination towards hill stations. But if truth be told, the place was quaint and very charming.

I headed for upper Coonoor where Venkat's grandparents owned a cottage called Honeysuckle Views. Once away from central Coonoor, which was a bustling, honking mess, I was relishing the cool air and the sheer romance of the city. Good place to meet up with Venkat, I thought. It also helped dispel my nervousness of meeting his family. As it were, Ma had flooded me with advice on how to present myself as a good and potential daughter-in-law, all of which made me sick.

Venkat's grandparents were a charming couple, full of warmth. I was also meeting Venkat after a long gap. We made a charmed circle with the older couple actively encouraging us to get away and be together. It didn't appear that they were scrutinizing me or vetting me or clearing me as a potential partner. They were merely accepting me with open arms and made me feel like a member of their family.

At lunch I met up with some cousins of Venkat. It was a blast. The cousins were visiting from Mumbai and overseas, and were so different from the crowd I am used to meeting. No hang-ups, no pretensions and nothing remotely sarkari or officious about them. It was clear that Venkat came from a pretty well-known family of that area, and they were well-to-do. The cousins sat around the dining table gently ribbing Venkat, teasing him about our imminent marriage. Raising a toast they chorused, 'Another one bites the dust!'

'No! No! No!' shouted another. 'The most stubborn bachelor amongst us bites the dust!'

There was laughter and general merriment around the table as we tucked in some awesome South Indian food.

I figured out after some time that Venkat was the only bureaucrat in that bunch. One of them ran a brewery from Coonoor while another was an event manager for celebrity dogs! I'd not heard of such fun professions in my life. Back home people became teachers or joined banks or took up government jobs and few, very few moved towards non-mainstream professions. Another cousin wa a researcher working on genetics and was at the receiving end of mild banter that he didn't earn a penny and was yet the hardest working amongst the cousins! All of this was a revelation for me. The people I met seemed to be doing what they wanted to do and were also enjoying it.

Two days into this and I was spoiled for life.

I told Venkat so.

'Everyone looks so free in your family, Venkat. I love their approach and their carefree orientation.'

He just grinned and said, 'No paradise is without trouble. Always. So don't get taken up by what you see. My cousins are happy in what they are doing whereas I'm satisfied with my life and so be it.'

'But look at us? They will like earn more, live life more, do what they want to. Whereas us? We'll be consigned to a dull life working at another person's bidding and effectively operating at the behest of someone else.'

But talking was the last thing Venkat wanted to do. He had other things on his mind. So that was that.

As we prepared to leave the next morning, Venkat's grandmother sought me out alone. The men were out, so that was not really difficult. She cleared her throat as though embarrassed about what she was going to say, but finally launched into the topic with a gush.

'You know, we wanted to tell you something about Venkat,' she said, 'you need to know more about him and what he is before you get married.'

'Sure,' I responded.

'He may have told you that his parents had a broken marriage. They never divorced but lived apart. You see, his mother, our daughter, was like a peacock, gorgeous and glamorous. Always obsessed with herself. She was and still is a classical dancer of repute. My husband forced her into this marriage, and we felt that as her husband was a diplomat, she would get the kind of lifestyle that would suit her personality.'

I was wrapped in the conversation and began wondering where it would lead to. Never ever had Venkat discussed his parents with me. It was always his grandparents that he spoke of. I mean I knew that his parents lived abroad, but that his mother was a world famous dancer and that his parents were estranged was never told to me.

'Well,' she continued, 'the marriage was short-lived and my daughter ended up having affairs with every conceivable person. Posting abroad became a nightmare because she would flit like a butterfly from man to man without a care or concern for her husband or the family. Finally Venkat was born. We thought that would tie her down but no! She whizzed off in three months, leaving him behind with us. According to her, she and a child were poles apart. So we brought him up. He was a quiet child but confident, and it helped that in the large joint family structure like ours he grew up amongst cousins and uncles and aunts with no shortage of love.'

Her eyes welled up in tears as she continued, 'We were desperate for him to settle down with someone he loved. I hated his choice of career as it took him so far away from us. But the boy has always been determined to be a bureaucrat and there was no overruling him on that choice.'

'Where are his parents?'

'His father is in Rangoon and will retire by next year. Our daughter moves from place to place giving performances. We see little of her but now, to our happiness, Venkat and his father have built a strong relationship. In fact, after retirement his father will move next door, to the adjacent cottage.'

I was pretty surprised. Venkat was a surprise package of many things: an estranged and famous mother, a large brood of unconventional cousins, a childhood spent in the rolling surroundings of Coonoor. Was all of this not so very remote and distinct from my staid, plodding life of Bareilly?

However, we had to catch our flight. Both of us were leaving together, and we left in a flurry of goodbyes. Venkat was heading to his current place of posting, and I for Dehradun to report for my first ever real job.

40

NO RELATIONSHIP IS PERFECT

'Venkat...,' I went in the flight.

'Hmm.'

'Listen...'

Silence. Then he simply said, 'Ask, you are obviously bursting with something.'

'As though I am that simple to read!'

'Arre... it's a compliment.'

So I asked him about his parents. His eyes shut immediately. The relaxed pose vanished as he turned towards window. After a while he caught my hand and told me that I was never ever to talk of his parents or raise the issue.

'Why?' I asked. 'You know everything about me and my family. Why this approach to your family?'

Venkat stared for long out of the aircraft and then quietly said, 'I have a father. But I am not too sure about my mother. Whatever you have heard of my parents while visiting my family may be true. But I will discuss this with you only when I am prepared to do so. You have met the people who have raised me and that should be enough for you to have confidence in our relationship.'

So be it. There was enough time in the flight for me to recap my journey with Venkat. He had almost grown into my being and become part and parcel of my life. Admittedly, it took a while for the romance to flower but by then he had become a key component of my existence; lock, stock and barrel. And if he didn't want to talk then he didn't. How did it matter? Although, can I say that like lock and key we were one piece, like filter and tobacco we were a single item? Why contemplate and why worry. After all, no relationship is perfect.

So I put my head on his shoulder and snoozed clutching at his hand.

41

ANOTHER NAIL IN MY COFFIN

*D*ear bad luck, was my immediate thought, let's break up! I landed for my first posting at Dehradun only to discover that the establishment officer who would determine my future was none other than the officer I had trained under at Rishikesh. My goose was pretty much cooked, and sure enough, he posted me far away, in the relative interior, at Pithoragarh. However, to give the man his due, he was pleasant. In fact, he made a big deal that I had been favoured by being posted in that district as it was a popular tourist destination.

It was a journey spanning over 450 kilometres by road, involving more than eight hours of driving over tortuous curves and bends. At the end of it I was in sheer utter despair due to motion sickness and threw up along the way. How different was this from my trip to Coonoor. My ever so helpful bitchy batchmates had informed me that normally this district was given to those who were out of favour with the administration. Had I done something to ruffle feathers that I was posted here?

As for Venkat, I guess he treated everything and my posting with his normal approach, that it was an experience and a positive one at that. He advised me to read the local newspapers, check out the district details and work out my local inspections. Fat load of good that would be to me! I mean I'm not much of a nature lover, and the chatty driver informed me that Pithoragarh was essentially a small town, a really small town, albeit prettily dotted with villages. It was in a valley, which meant that whichever inspection I did would be up and down the mountains. Even the driver could foresee that it would be tough for me. The internet search was also not encouraging: some restaurants, a couple of cyber cafes. That was that.

I was hanging on the slender hope on what the future held; once Venkat and I fixed the wedding date, I'd be out of the place and maybe out of the state too.

We reached the city, which was breathtakingly pretty, though that just didn't register on me. The car went straight to my residence, a massive, British era building of two floors. I could spot a large, shabby and careworn house in the centre of the gardens. My instinctive thought: am I walking towards something I should be running away from? With limited options, I entered the place. The ground floor had a gigantic fire place and was probably built for hosting parties and gatherings. Up the wooden staircase I reached a landing which led to three rooms, cavernous and crammed with teak furniture.

How on earth was I to live here? I would be a skeleton rattling on a tin roof in all this space. The house was freezing, although winter was still a few months away. I chose the smallest bedroom for myself, and entering it broke into a fit of sneezing. The wretched bedding had definitely not been aired in years. The sheets were filthy and I was back to the training days at Rishikesh; summoning staff to air the bedding and being told that as the sun was setting it would be of no use. So I set out to the market and bought myself bedding, some sheets and a shawl. Not to mention a toilet cleaner and acid for the filthy toilet bowl.

Back at my residence, with no desire as yet to call it home, I hit the sack. What I hadn't reckoned for was the moonlight which continuously streamed into the room from the window set high above, near the ceiling. And if that were not disturbing enough, the wretched house creaked and groaned through the night, and I sat up most of the time petrified that ghosts of the long gone British era were enjoying themselves in my allotted accommodation. At night the shapes changed. The room was different: bigger, blacker and longer. Every creak of the wooden staircase and every groan in the floorboards sent me into a fit. And that was my first night at Pithoragarh, a pretty much miserable introduction to the place.

The training days had pretty much instilled in me the pattern of government offices; there was little point in reaching office before 10 a.m. Groggily, I decided to walk to the place just to while away time.

Well, even when office began, it was little different from my Rishikesh days, except this time I was the boss sitting on the right side of the table and staring across at the photograph of the president and the chief minister in a hideously painted room. To add to the general sense of interior decoration gone totally wrong, a few grimy phone instruments in various colours adorned the green baize of my table. Giving them company was the ubiquitous brass vase, in which rested a few plastic flowers. Where on earth do I start from? The house allotted to me or this room? I needed to create some space to call my comfort zone.

One of the phones buzzed. It was the filthiest instrument,

off white and coated in greasy. I didn't pick it given its state of filth. The buzz was insistent. In a while the peon came running in to tell me that the chief minister was on line and I should hurry up and take the call. Using a handkerchief to cover the mouthpiece, I spoke into the receiver.

'Good morning, Sir.'

'Namaskar. To aapne join kar liya (You have joined)?'

'Yes, Sir.'

'Dekhiye, apni district se parichai kar lijiye jaldi se (Please familiarize yourself with the district). I am deputing my Minister for Secondary Education to pay a visit and inspect your area. You have a capable senior, Negi, whom you will be reporting to. It will be good for you to immediately pick up things from him.'

I stared at the phone for a while after the call was over. Next I called for a bottle of Colin to clean that dratted phone before I got down to the task of figuring out how to familiarize myself with my district.

The Colin never came. (It required a note to be put in a file, then my approval, then the Accounts Department to release the funds and finally the purchase!) Meanwhile, Venkat helped me to go about things and I got to work in gusto. Gusto, as much as Pithoragarh timing permitted. One o' clock came and everyone pushed off for lunch. As sitting alone in a deserted office was no fun, I too headed back for my house, getting into a state of panic about the impending night. I lay in my bed, on my new mattress and just drifted off to sleep. It was dark when I woke up totally disoriented. Damn, it was already five in the evening!

I rushed to work. Obviously, everyone had left, barring my PA who gleefully informed that the Minister for Secondary

Education had called, and that I had missed the video conferencing with the chief minister that happened daily at four in the evening. Not nice, not at all nice. I needed to re-work my strategy. I needed to look at settling in fast and being in command of things, before my poor reputation in the state spread even to some place as remote as Pithoragarh.

For starters, I befriended my PA and asked for a detailed list of people who worked under me. Next, I made off to meet my boss who was a promoted IAS officer. He was a local person, close to retirement. I was happy to meet the man; he appeared kind, genial and very concerned about my journey from Dehradun, and also the creaking house. I was promptly invited over for dinner to his house, which I gladly accepted. It didn't help that my PA had casually mentioned that a grave rested in the compound of my house.

'A grave?!'

'Yes, Madam.'

'How on earth can I live in a house with a grave?'

'No, Madam, it is in the garden not in the house.'

Hello??!! Was this guy playing games with me? He amplified that it was the grave of a dog called Patricia who had died in 1916. Her owner had interred her body in the garden. Maybe I could check out the tombstone when I took a round of the place, he suggested?

There was no way I'd go back to the house until I got over the shock of having to live with the ghost of a dog. Office over, I went across to the nearest market and indulged in random shopping, all the while petrified of the night ahead.

My fear got the better of me. I confessed to my boss and his wife, seeking a solution. It was decided that their daughter would stay with me temporarily until a local lady was found to be with me at least during the night. Of course, I knew by now that this new development would reach Dehradun and become yet another nail in my coffin!

I wept that night and wept some more when Venkat called and continued sniffling into my pillow until I became weary and dozed off.

42

BREAKING NEWS!

*B*reaking news! 'Babu sacked for wearing ten rings!' screamed the headlines in the local papers. Everyone in the office was abuzz with the news that an official had been sacked in the adjoining district by none other than the minister who was to inspect our district. According to reports, the minister found several irregularities during his inspection of the office of the district inspector of schools. He summoned the accounts officer who greeted him with folded hands. The minister saw the rings on the officer's fingers and shouted, 'How can you wear so many expensive rings on your fingers? There has to be some scam in this.' He then immediately asked the district in-charge officer to suspend the accounts officer and initiate an inquiry against him.

Everyone around was left dazed. How could wearing ten rings be a ground for suspension? Even my boss looked nervous. The official version whitewashed the incident, but we were now really wary. Realistically, I should be out of the loop having just joined, but the chief minister had called me about the visit, so I guess I was very much in the loop. Nothing made sense to me, I didn't even know my way around the office, but

I guess I had hit the ground running and run I had to at a really fast pace!

Well, the next day was full of frenzy. It began with us lining up to greet the minister with garlands, bouquets and sweet smiles plastered on our faces. Yet again I was in a sari which was threatening to fall off despite half a dozen pins holding it in place. The minister immediately began his inspection of the office and then chose a small school and a hospital for the next inspection. In between, we broke for refreshments. The four of us; the minister, his PA, my boss and I went to a room with over-sized sofas to tuck into steaming chai and samosas and cashew nuts. Much later in my bureaucratic journey I figured out that cashew nuts were served on really special occasions, and that only 5 or 6 of these were served on a plate to a person unless, of course, one was a VIP. Normally, one never got second helpings. But as for now, I took neither chai nor snacks, dreading as I were that some bouncer would be posed at me or worse, that if I stood, my sari would fall off!

While I was ignored, it was a great opportunity to watch Negi, my boss, greasing the minister! The man was a professional at the art and the minister stood no chance at even getting a single word in. To everything the minister said, Negi would knowledgably nod and say, 'Haan ji, Sir; Of Course, Sir; Ho jayaga, Sir.' He inundated the minister with figures and facts which no one could really verify; the minister was captured to his sofa chair in a way that would leave little time for any detailed or useful inspection. Sun and time both set early in these parts, and Negi had lined up a cultural programme in the evening. There would be little time to spare for criticisms or worse, suspensions.

Eventually, he persuaded the minister to inspect a school

campus close by, as well as the spot where a student had been molested recently. The sleepy and harmonious place that Pithoragarh was, it was a rarity that such incidents even happened. But it had and the minister had no choice but to agree; the press had been lined up for the inspection. We were greeted by students who sang a rehearsed prayer and then proceeded to demonstrate their versatility in song and dance. Over-painted kids performed on Bollywood numbers, a hugely nauseating experience for me. A little later, the minister addressed the students and teachers and condemned the incident saying that security to all the educational institutions in the state was his top priority and that any sort of criminal activities inside the campus would not be tolerated. Whosoever found guilty should be befittingly punished according to the law of the land. He also disclosed, to loud applause, that the accused involved in the crime was arrested last week. Then came the highlight of his speech: he announced that the incident had happened because there was no proper school boundary and that he was committed to construct a boundary wall. The hapless engineer accompanying us was thereafter directed to repair the dilapidated campus roads of the school within a week.

He made off amidst thunderous applause and lots of cheers—leaving us in peace, duly abandoning the cultural show for something better.

Negi was thrilled and he insisted that I accompany him for a celebratory dinner home. Venkat and I had fixed up time to Skype. Also, I was dying to get out of the sari. But boss is boss, and I reluctantly joined another officer in the car en route to his house.

'So,' asked my companion, 'how was your first exposure to a minister's inspection?'

'Great! Simply great! The minister is such a committed person. Look at how he addressed the school and directed the engineer to ensure that the boundary wall gets constructed. I was really impressed. As for Mr Negi, now I can understand why he is so popular and respected in these parts.'

The man gave me a quizzical look. 'Are you innocent or naive or what?' He retorted. 'This site has been inspected three times by three different ministers who have all given three different targets. This molestation incident was off campus, and an incident that had nothing to do with the school or its children. It's just been hyped as an incident involving the school kids and now the lie has become the so-called truth.'

My jaw dropped. Isn't this the stuff of breaking news? This couldn't be true. But it seemingly was so. My companion continued, 'Look, you are inexperienced and more so being a woman is a huge handicap. Guys pick up these things better. At the end of the day, everyone will benefit, Negi too, and maybe a small wall will also come up as elections are close by.'

'But,' I spluttered, 'the minister assured that the money will be released.'

'Oh, don't doubt that bit. The money will most certainly be released, like it was earlier, for building a protective fencing around the school. Actually, let me explain to you how it works here. I had accompanied Negi for a trip abroad. Our host, the province governor, lived in real style and Negi complimented him so. Later, at the governor's house, after downing a few drinks, our host couldn't stop boasting about how the bridge across the river which we could view from his living room partly belonged to him. When he did a reciprocal trip to India, Negi hosted him in equal measure. The man was impressed and it was his turn to quiz Negi about how he managed to live in such a manner, despite being a government servant. Negi took him to his living room window and asked him to view the bridge over the stream across. The governor was puzzled because there was no bridge, only a stream. 'That's the point,' Negi laughed rousingly 'that there is no bridge and it all belongs to me.'

Funny. And now I am going to dine with this guy who eats up all the money that rightfully should have been spent on a bridge. I was quite dismayed and called up Venkat much later at night to moan about it. He seemingly had a different career trajectory in these last few weeks, which partly had prevented us from pursuing our wedding goal with the speed I had contemplated. He had been identified as a bright spark, and was assigned a posting to handle the finances of his state. Only the best and brightest were ever given that job. Obviously, his world vision would be different. After I cribbed over the phone for a longish while, he told me to drop it, go to sleep and not really rely on tales someone else was carrying.

No consolation that. My silent conclusion was that this was the worst possible discovery for me: my job sucked, totally sucked and, I was a total misfit.

43

A SECRET

I decided to wade through my Pithoragarh days with the small flicker of hope that the entire situation was temporary. Meanwhile, I passed my solitary evenings re-connecting with old friends on social media, a lot of whom seemed to have gone abroad. They'd swoon that I was in Pithoragarh. 'How romantic!' Isn't it the gateway to Mansarovar,' one of them asked. Another assured me that on her next visit to India she'd make my home a base while trekking through the Himalayas. Misraji also reappeared in my life. Perhaps only he figured out what it meant for me be all by myself, far away from Venkat, going through the ordeals of becoming an IAS officer. I warmed up to him immensely.

Then one day, out of the blue, I saw a comment from Deepak, my college mate. He had reacted to something on another friend's post and I randomly I sent him a friend request to confirm that it was really him. And hey! There I was, in touch with Deepak. The last that Deepak and I had met was with his foreign lady love. So, I asked him about her.

'No more on the scene,' was his limited reply. 'What about you? Have you found someone?'

'Yes. A service colleague.'

'Love?'

'Of course! Nothing less than love for me.'

'Great! And how are you finding the job? Have you found the stars you were dreaming of? Somehow, between us guys we'd always discuss how you, amongst the girls, were so hung up on this exam, that if nothing else then your focus would carry you to the IAS.'

'Well', I responded, and throwing caution to the winds and speaking more openly than I would have to any other, 'it's not all that great at the end of the day. More hype than substance. As for the dream, it was for the most part my father's and not mine.'

'So yours waits for you still...' he wrote.

I took a deep breath and then finally admitted to him and to myself, 'Yes, mine still waits for me.'

Having confessed that, I was relieved. The job was not up my alley. And who in any case dreams of becoming a government servant these days? All my erstwhile college mates seemed to be doing something or another which they had wanted to do, while I was stuck at Pithoragarh chumming up to the likes of Negi and living in a house with a grave. The only thing I'd learnt so far was that I was a total misfit in this place and my job.

Late at night came another message from Deepak, 'Remember that the snow goose does not need to bathe to make it white. Be yourself and you'll be easy.'

Frustration has strange reactions on the mind. In my case, I see light only when frustrated, which is what led me to request Venkat to buy me a camera. Venkat being Venkat, did his bit of research and bought me a hugely expensive piece with three zoom lens. It reached me in no time, courtesy the bureaucratic network. I got down mastering it and whiling away my time in a more productive manner than at the office. I also got down to blogging regularly. Adopting an alias, I'd post little bits about the Uttarakhand hills. It was my little secret, kept away from Venkat too. Enrolling for an online course in photography, my photos and casual writing became my getaway from the mundane. I started posting photos on various photography sites and was delighted with the viewer hits and comments. Casually, I recommended my blog to the college crowd. It was an alias, so I was certain that my secret would remain with me.

The nights became delicious as I wrote, edited my photos and got totally immersed in a new world. In fact, overcoming my desire to retch each time I got into a car and started touring the hills extensively, my camera my constant companion.

It was a new me, a lovely, beautiful discovery. The feeling that I got when I was with Jojo. He and I were made for each other. We knew each other. I could say or do anything foolish and yet he'd tilt his head with a look that'd say 'My god! I never thought of that!' With an indiscriminate, undemanding knowledge of me, he understood my language, and vice versa. The camera was the same. It responded to my love and was much more than an object for me. It would perform miracles.

The government had given me a laptop. I upgraded its memory card and connected it to the laptop so that I could the see the results of my camera shots immediately. I was in love. Totally in love. The birds, the sunset, the people, the stray dogs, they captivated me no end as I relentlessly clicked. Once, passing by a hamlet, I lost balance jumping out of the car to click at an old person, wrinkled, toothless, yet happiness writ over his face.

That evening I posted that on my blog. Lots of hits and then a ping came on my WhatsApp.

'Hey! Is that you who is running that blog on the hills?'

It was Deepak.

'Why?'

'Okay, that answers my question. So it is you. Well done! I love your photographs.'

'Look. Don't tell anyone. It's my secret. And I want to keep it that way. No one knows.'

'Not even your fiancée?'

'Nope. Look, you just keep this to yourself. Who I tell and who I don't tell is purely my concern.'

'But a secret from the man you love? Remember what Gandhi said about marriage? That there should be no secrets between husbands and wives. They are one in two or two in one.'

'What kind of wonky ideas do you have?! And Gandhi today is outdated...'

'So, Madam, do I understand that you and your lover have not merged into each other?'

Irritable, I cut him off and swore to block his messages. He was invasive and had figured out a part of me that was just evolving. How on earth had he done so was a mystery. I had in fact sent the link of my blog to Venkat as well. But he had either not seen it or not connected it with me. And this guy, whom I hardly knew, had established a connection sitting zillions of miles away!

Venkat called up shortly after to let me know that he was close to getting a fix on the process for our cadre change after marriage. He'd found a fellow officer who assured that things could be fast forwarded shortly after we got hitched. Still seething over my interaction with Deepak, I just waded through the conversation, hardly muttering a word.

'What's up with you?' He asked. 'I am talking of our life.'

'Nothing. Just that everything seems so like having to be worked out and organized. I mean if we mean to marry then why does the government has to come into the picture?

'Because darling, we are in the government. It is our employer and come whatever, we cannot be together unless we go through the process.'

'Yeah, but it takes away from the thrill of impulse. I mean, like, okay we are in love and we want to marry and then comes all the planning and the procedure, which you keep on telling me about, which makes me feel that the entire thing is a real wretched burden.'

Long silence. Venkat responded by saying goodnight and cutting the line. I got an SMS from him a minute later. He said that he was pretty convinced by now that I tended to see things from a very limited perspective and that I should learn to broaden my world view. I tried calling him back and found the phone switched off. Most of the night was spent in going over what he had said and what on earth he had meant by what he said. In the end, I confessed to myself that I was extremely hurt.

44

BE CAREFUL OF WHOSE TOES
YOU STEP ON

Shortly thereafter I was summoned to Dehradun. Normally no one bothers to call any officer across from Pithoragarh, given its distance, and makes do with only urgent trips. But this time, I was asked to undertake the long drive to the headquarters and meet the establishment officer, the same person who I had trained under at Rishikesh.

The drive was fun as I had carried my camera. Venkat was to meet me at Dehradun with Baba for finalizing our wedding plans. At the Circuit House I found only Baba. Venkat had been held back at work by another day, and we had a magnificent reunion. I wasn't senti, but yes, I did feel a sense of warmth in Baba's company. He was discerning in noticing that I was disenchanted in my response to work. He tried probing but got only monosyllabic replies.

'How are things at work?'

'Okay.'

'Are you comfortable now? I can imagine that the initial days would have been tough and lonely. Your mother and I were also very upset that they had posted you so far away. Particularly, as you are a girl and a single one at that.'

'Forget it, Baba!' I snapped. 'Everyone has to go through the grind. I'm better for the experience. And what is all this girl-shirl business? They will post me wherever a vacancy exists.'

Baba went quiet for a while but couldn't resist saying that he felt a change in me. I looked at peace with myself and certainly more confident, unlike before.

'Really?' I asked. 'Maybe it was the experience of living by myself in such quiet surroundings and fending for myself.'

Then I showed him some of my photographs, which I could figure out didn't capture his interest one bit. So we resorted to small chit-chat. The passion of my life, which had seen me through the last few months, remained unstated between us. Though my mind was ablaze with one thought: of the three people who mattered most to me in the world; Baba, Ma and Venkat, all had failed to recognize my talent and newfound love. In contrast, a relative stranger, miles away, had fathomed and identified my aptitude in this direction. In fact, just before leaving Pithhoragrah he had even sent me a mail that one of the photos that I had posted should be sent for a competition.

Next day was my meeting with the establishment officer. I could frankly care two hoots any more, my disillusionment with bureaucracy was complete. A sycophant boss who used his wife to suck up to his political master and another who had sold his soul for corruption was enough to get one's goat. Gone was the meek me, and in place was sheer absolute indifference. I wasn't looking at superior beings but was seeing them as locusts, parasites of the system called the Great Indian Bureaucracy. Baba had been wrong. There was no power in here, only abuse and misuse of position. I was yet to figure out what was the real power in life, but for sure, it did not lie in this wretched creaky set-up.

The officer greeted me enthusiastically. This was okay as he was a pleasant sort, handicapped only with a vicious social climber for a wife. Add ambition to that and they are made for each other. We exchanged pleasantries. He served me my favourite tea, which he remembered from the training days, and then threw me off course by asking, 'So you are getting married?'

I merely nodded.

'To Venkat? Bright boy. The brightest the service has seen in years. He'll go a long way.'

Again I nodded as there was really not much to say to that. That Venkat is bright is an irrefutable fact. He cleared his throat next and actually looked embarrassed when he asked, 'I remember he came to visit you when you were training under me. But I didn't connect the dots then. So, where did you meet him? I mean, I understand that it is a love marriage and …'

I chose to ignore him and merrily sipped at my tea. Now, the guy was totally embarrassed out of his wits and I enjoyed watching that.

'You know, when I told my wife about your marriage, she was rather happy and we were discussing how both of you got around to meeting each other.'

As I'd finished my tea and the gent had squirmed enough, I decided to relieve him of his discomfort.

'We met here and there.'

'But if you look at it, there is so much difference between both of you. Like he is from the south and has an international education. Do you know that his uncle is a top ranking officer in the Government of India? You know, the person who works with the prime minister...'

Not that I knew that bit but the first part of the remark had annoyed me no end. I decided to restrict my reply to that bit alone.

'Sir, how we met and what differences there are between us is something to be sorted out by us. So long as we are happy, I don't see how it should affect anyone else.'

Long silence. There was nothing left to say. In fact, had I been in his place, I'd have closed the conversation there and then but this guy was by now a combo of anger and discomfiture, which made him warble into more words.

'Look, I am rather fond of you and it would be good if you give a serious thought to my words. Learn from Venkat and restrain your impulsive nature. That will hold you in good stead in the future.'

Once again I opted for silence, which brought an end to our little meeting. I trotted out, peacefully leaving behind a squirming mass of flesh, wrath and irritation. Hah! I thought! There goes the sucker who was probably chumming up to me because of Venkat's highly placed connections. Holding back a smile, I restrained the impulse to tell him to be careful of whose toes you step on today, for they might be attached to the ass you have to kiss tomorrow!

45

MY GOOSE WAS ROYALLY COOKED

I found Venkat at the Circuit House. His natural query was about my meeting with the establishment officer and the purpose of my being in Dehradun.

'How did it go?'

'How do you think it went?'

'Hey! What's up? Look, I'm asking you something and you're replying with a question. How on earth would I know how your meeting went?'

'Oh, drop it Venkat.'

'Hello? Drop what? What's up with you? Why this attitude? You should be happy that we are meeting after so long. Instead, you are seething with resentment. Frankly, I can't fathom you at all.'

'If you can't then you can't.'

Tears welled up and I tried moving towards my room to avoid any more unpleasant discussions. I needed that little bit of space to let myself calm down. Also, I was worried that Baba might be around and overhear our bickering. But Venkat was quicker than me. Catching my hand he remarked, 'Okay. Let's begin again. How about starting with a pleasant exchange of greetings?'

'I need to be alone Venkat. For a bit. Give me a break and we'll talk.'

Churlish of me, but such was my mood at that point of time. Baba wasn't back yet and I lay on the bed staring at the ceiling. Just staring, not thinking. I had done enough of thinking being by myself at Pithoragarh. Something snapped in me. The overwhelming guilt of being someone in the eyes of my father and following a destiny so mapped out for me, and subsequently buffeted by a relationship with Venkat had suddenly disappeared. I felt a sense of vacuum. And yes, one of relief too.

Venkat knocked at the door and entered my room. He looked unsure as to what would follow.

'We need to talk and should do so before your father returns.'

I maintained silence. So he drew up a chair close to the bed and reached out for my hand. 'Look, I don't know what happened today but you have to tell me. These situations are common in government workings. Give things time. After all, no two days are the same...'

'I told you earlier Venkat. Drop it. Please. I can't explain anything to you.'

'Try me.'

'Like how? Where do I start from?'

'Tell me what happened at work today for a start. Please howl at me. Please scream. Please speak for god's sake. We are a couple. A couple in love. And the thing about loving someone is that you can yell at them if it feels good to do so. Tomorrow we'll be moving on to our places of posting and by then if we don't sort this out, all we'll do is take this silent resentment back.'

So I asked Venkat what exactly he was achieving by hiding his great bureaucratic associations from me. Sore with the odious public perception that he was a better person than me, I asked him if he was aware that it was common talk in the bureaucratic circles.

'Where on earth has this become an issue between what is strictly a relationship between you and me?'

'It's not.'

But now that I had started there was no stopping. I went hammer and tongs at him for hiding things from me. That he was always preaching at me. That he treated me like a kid and not an adult. All type of resentful things poured out. He was quite dazed. Frankly, so was I by the fact that I was carrying so much of anger in me. I think I reacted like a crazy person, something frankly unwarranted with the situation. But a dam had seemingly burst within me.

After a long while I stopped, the words hanging between us in the air.

'I don't understand this thinking of yours,' Venkat tried reasoning after a while. 'What's the trigger?'

'What do you understand of me at all, Venkat? Do you know how lonely I have been all these months? On top of that, getting exposed to the sheer nonsense of Indian bureaucracy. Where were you all this while? You kept on telling me that things will change. We will get married. Give yourself time, and so on and so forth. You know what? If you had these great uncles in the system then why didn't you figure out a way for us to get married earlier?'

'That's unfair,' Venkat reacted. 'You'd asked for time and it was only right for me to respect that.'

'Venkat. Let me put it plain and proper. I think bureaucracy and me are poles apart. Baba had a dream for me which I somehow fulfilled. Your support was there. But it may have been better if I'd been warned that there was no great euphoric experience waiting for me out there.'

'What can I say? Which job is so enchanting that it sends you to cloud nine? Problems exist everywhere.'

'Maybe. But why don't you realize that I never explored other options. I never had my own dreams. I never did what I wanted to do. There's an all new world waiting out there, Venkat. In this day and age, you can go about experimenting. Stability, power and all that jazz are dead.'

I had uttered enough hurtful things. I had also revealed enough of my confusion to Venkat. There were no answers. In any case we couldn't talk more because Baba had returned, and the evening ended that way. I had to take that long drive back the next day. So we had an early dinner and called it a night.

All night I lay awake, listening to Baba's gentle snores, thinking, correctly perhaps, that my goose was cooked. Right royally cooked. I had no future in the small hopeless world of Uttarakhand bureaucracy. A reputation of sorts had developed about me, which was wholly unflattering, and I would pretty much have to learn to live with that. The chances that this image about me would carry to the next place of posting were really strong. Venkat and I would forever be called a couple comprising a 'nice man and his wretched wife'!

46

BETTER SENSE PREVAILS

We went and filed our papers in the registrar's office despite the events of last night. I mechanically went ahead and did that. There was utter confusion in my mind but until I resolved things for myself, mustering the courage to tell Baba anything would take time.

I headed for Pithoragarh. During the long drive, there was adequate time to mull, mull and indulge in more mull. Yes, I had come to an end of a defining phase in my life. The last three years had passed in a blur of studies, and labour to achieve the goal of becoming an IAS officer. I had walked into a job which was simply unappealing. And the fact was that all the while when I was a kid wanting to grow older and fulfill my dreams, this shit was not what I had expected! But had I grown up at all? It was time to sort all of that: Maybe it was time now to re-invent, to re-think priorities and chase a different dream, a dream that was mine alone. And once I discovered my dream, all I had to do was to follow it. Happiness lay in that, perhaps.

As the car moved on, I too moved on with my thoughts, until finally free of them, I dozed off into a state of blessed slumber where the confusions would neither intrude nor would I have to struggle with myself. Only one niggle remained: what would be Venkat's role in my new thinking? Only time would tell, I thought lazily, and slowly dozed off. In this frame of mind the future looked attractive. Frankly, I didn't mind going nowhere as long as it would be an interesting path.

I was jolted out of my sleep with a jerk. There was a massive landslide on the route and my car had to be diverted. Reckoning that a break in journey was inevitable, I headed towards Rishikesh to stay over the night. Despite all the experiences I had earlier undergone, it was a nice, comfortable feeling to enter the Circuit House and meet Grumpy and others. I dug out my camera and headed towards the Ganges in pursuit of good shots. I felt a change in me. Now I was more confident, more sure and definitely not so diffident in stepping out on my own to explore and discover new sights and sounds.

Ping went my mobile. A pleasant surprise awaited me! Deepak was in these parts and was a leap and jump away at some resort close by undergoing a detox therapy.

'Arre,' I typed, 'how come you never told me that you were heading for India?'

'It was a sudden programme. My law firm sent me out to Delhi and I thought of combining this bit of travel with my India tour.'

'I'm just ten-odd kilometres away,' I replied. 'Should we meet?'

'Most certainly! How about dinner? You can join me at the resort and partake of the detox diet!'

So we fixed up a time. All this while, I had studiously avoided Venkat's calls and was even contemplated blocking him temporarily from my contact list. There was a burning desire inside me to simply avoid him until I was sure what I was up to and to where I was heading. Talking to him might weaken my thinking and cloud my decisions.

Meeting Deepak was a delight! We chatted nineteen to the dozen. I displayed my portfolio of photographs to him and he had a suggestion that I take a break soon to do a course in photography in the US. There and then he gave me a solution to my dilemma of what next. Things were moving really fast. My mind was churning. All in a span of a day I had registered for a wedding to a man with whom I was now doubting a lifelong commitment, I was wanting to move on and out of my job. I was seriously in a rebel mode. Deepak appeared as a saviour, some sort of a knight in shining armour. As the hours progressed and we sat out under the starry night, he began acquiring shades of something that was turning into an attraction. Who knows how the evening had started and who knows how the night would end? Yes, I was in dangerous territory and walking a path without care or concern, but it was situational.

Better sense prevailed though; I finally and reluctantly choose to end the evening. Deepak and I made our way out. The night was clear and the stars were twinkling. The chill had not yet set in. It was a lovely evening.

'Let's walk a bit more,' Deepak suggested.

'It's getting late...' I demurred but continued on with his suggestion.

I don't know when we moved closer, but there it was, we were in a tight embrace, throwing caution to the winds.

'You are one hell of an attractive dame,' muttered Deepak. 'And I'm sorry I couldn't control myself. I know that you are engaged to be married but...'

'Well, it was not as though I was unwilling, it takes two to tango. So don't blame yourself alone.'

'And your fiancé?'

I kept quiet. What about Venkat? Clearly I was two-timing and my mind was in a wrestle. I wasn't thinking straight and had lost power over rational thinking. Why on earth had Deepak brought Venkat's reference into the conversation? Things had turned awkward now. As swift as the emotions had built up between us, they drained out too, leaving me sans passion.

I moved away and let the moment pass without a reply. We parted. Clutching at my laptop, I got into the car and made off for the Circuit House.

I sat out in the garden for the remainder of the night, thinking. What on earth had I been thinking? I hardly knew the guy, except as someone whom I had met on and off in my life. Yet, without thought or care, what type of signals had I given him? Was I just escaping from what I perceived as a seemingly hopeless situation? Till a few hours ago I was merely a girl on the cusp of becoming someone modelled by the desires and fancies of my family. A girl who may not know what she wanted. Someone who did not know who she was. I think I deserved the chance to find out. Actually, when one is young, say seventeen, the right thing to do is so easy to see because one doesn't have to make any big decisions. One knows that no matter what one does, someone will fix everything. But when one is all grown up, the world is not that black and white, and the right thing doesn't have a tidy little arrow pointing to it.

All of a sudden I'd grown up. Maybe I'd been growing up in bits and pieces for quite some time now, without actually knowing about it. In the process I'd found that growing up can mean a lot of things. Most importantly, it meant that I had to make reasonable choices and not take knee-jerk decisions. It did not imply totally discarding the old and declaring to myself that I had become somebody completely new and stop loving the things I used to love. It just meant that I've added more things to my list to love and live with.

Only a kid behaves peevishly like I had been doing. All this while I had been growing older but not growing up.

It was early morning when I chose to drive towards the devastated area from which I had turned away the day before. Unprecedented rains had triggered flash floods and severe landslides. There were mile long queues with people desperate in search of food and water. In the narrow roads, there was no way that a vehicle could be turned back. People were desperately waiting for relief. In this situation I was someone who could do something, someone with authority, someone who the district administration would respond to. I got out of the car. The driver cautioned that I could be facing the crowd's anger as a result of the frustration of waiting and hunger. But well, I needed to do something. Venkat's words were ringing in my ears; this was why I was in the IAS, so that I could do something. Before I finally took the plunge of leaving the service which I had been seriously contemplating over the past few days, I needed to give myself a chance, just one more chance.

Close by, the rescue and rehabilitation teams had started reaching and introducing themselves. I too joined in mapping casualties, identifying the infants, the elderly and the sick who needed immediate attention, mobilizing the able-bodied as caregivers. I was fortunately carrying with me a fully charged mobile, which was used to connect people to their families. We worked through the day until finally, the first boulders were removed and the early traffic carrying the neediest could be moved. By the next morning, most of the stranded people had been sent off. Repairing the road would be a longer job for the local administration to oversee, but I could move on satisfied that there had been limited causalities and the deadly aftermath of the flash downpour resolved.

It was two nights that I had not slept, one on my account and the other while working at the site. Totally exhausted, I slept off in the car until we reached Pithoragarh. It was a deep and refreshing sleep, a sort of cleansing. I woke up rejuvenated to a fresh thinking. I saw the world now with my own eyes instead that of an escapist's. I finally saw the reality. Several situations had come into my life as blessings, but this situation had been different; it had come in as a lesson. I had done something worthwhile. I had finally got my act together to figure out what it was that triggered Venkat's thrill in this job. There was a lot to be learnt, and the learning for me, late instead of never, began now.

The phone trilled as I entered my house. I looked at it and smiled. It was Venkat. Thank god for him! Unquestioning, simple and accepting Venkat. His message read: 'Hope you are now ready to take my call. You did a marvellous job back there. Congratulations! I am really proud of you. The local media has covered your contribution in the relief work.'

'Thanks, teacher,' I replied. 'I owe it all to you. Don't know what you saw in me, but I have been such a baby.'

Venkat replied as only he could, 'Never say that. In fact, if I could give you one thing in life it would be the ability to see you through my eyes. Only then would you know how special you are to me, in whatever shape, whichever avatar'.

I don't know when it started, this relationship of ours—in the canteen, over a cup of tea, with a simple, 'hello'. I never thought it would lead to this. When was it that my mind had started to concentrate on this one person? When was it that the thought of him, talking to him, would dissipate my problems and replace them with butterflies and a smile? I had a good feeling.

I was back to being in love with this guy! I moved ahead into the house with confident strides, a different person from the uneasy fresher who had made her way in just a few months ago.